THE GARANSAY PRESS

THE DARK ISLE

DCI DANI BEVAN #10

BY

KATHERINE
PATHAK

D1601418

Books by Katherine Pathak

The Imogen and Hugh Croft Mysteries:

Aoife's Chariot

The Only Survivor

Lawful Death

The Woman Who Vanished

Memorial for the Dead
(Introducing DCI Dani Bevan)

The Ghost of Marchmont Hall

Short Story collection:

The Flawed Emerald and other Stories

DCI Dani Bevan novels:

Against A Dark Sky

On A Dark Sea

A Dark Shadow Falls

Dark as Night

The Dark Fear

Girls of The Dark

Hold Hands in the Dark

Dark Remedies

Dark Origin

The Dark Isle

Standalone novels:

I Trust You

4

© Katherine Pathak, 2017

#TheDarkIsle

Edited by: The Currie Revisionists, 2017

© Cover photograph Pixabay Images

Author's Note

The Isles of Ghiant and Nabb are purely fictitious and will not be found in the locations described.

Scotland's Small Isles consist of Rum, Eigg, Canna and Muck.

I hope you visit them one day.

Prologue

A family of otters had created a shelter amongst the remains of a stone wall. Twigs, sea grasses and mud had been packed tightly together in the gaps between the rocks. As night fell, their sleek bodies could be seen surfacing from the water, moving with swift stealth across the smooth sand towards their holt.

What had once been the shop and post office was now a haven for assorted wildlife that would have delighted any enthusiast. Shags and Guillemots were nesting in the chimneys, whilst bats had made their home amongst the rafters of the disintegrating cottage next door. In fact, the island was as full of life as it had ever been, in all its long history.

Except none of it was human any more.

On this perfect early Spring evening, things were no different. The wind had died down and only a thin wisp of cloud covered the sky as the sun set to a deep pink over the sea.

Dusk revealed the island's nocturnal inhabitants; including the black rats who, on this particular occasion, had found a reason to materialize in their dozens, congregating on the concrete floor of one of the barns which had once been part of the largest farm on Ghiant.

The rats had found something new to feed upon.

In the semi-darkness, their bodies moved almost in unison, feasting upon a fresh carcass, half hidden under a pile of damp straw. Their frantic activities brought in a swoop of gulls, keen to enjoy the pickings that this flurry of scavenging surely signalled. Their urgent squawks filled the evening sky and shattered the peace.

But there was no one to disturb. The otters were curled comfortably in their shelter, uninterested in the furore. They'd fed well that day on crabs and clams. The shoreline being rich territory for them without the fishermen's ubiquitous pots and lines.

The cries of the gulls on the still air soon abated. This rare disruption to the subtle ebbs and flows of the island had passed quickly. An eerie silence took its place. What was left of the body still lay on the barn floor. Soon, the growing darkness would have enveloped it completely, obscuring its presence in this remote location, where no living human made its home.

Chapter 1

A decision had been bothering Bill Hutchison all day. The quandary had almost spoiled the walk he and Joy had taken amongst the foothills of the Cuillin mountains. Which was a great shame, as the weather was clear and bright, with far-reaching views across the sound to Rum.

Upon their return to the modest guesthouse in Portree where they were staying, Bill vigorously brushed chunks of mud off their hiking boots, whilst perching on the back step. The owner kindly offered him a mug of peat brown tea whilst he worked.

"You were lucky with the weather today," Mrs Stewart commented idly.

"Aye," Bill replied with feeling. "It was our first proper walk of the holiday."

He twisted round to catch her eye. "And it seems set fair for the remainder of the week."

The lady smiled tolerantly. She was used to this kind of pre-occupation with the meteorological conditions of Skye from her residents, particularly the older ones.

Bill continued, "only I'd thought that with the wind settling down, we might visit some of the smaller islands."

Isla Stewart rested her weight on the door frame and took a sip of her own tea. "The Robertsons run a daily boat out to Rum and Nabb. You can spend a good few hours on either before returning to Skye. There are several nice wee cafés and shops to visit. The beaches are to die for."

Bill wrinkled his brow. "Aye, I'm aware of that particular service." He cleared his throat. "My interest was actually in the Isle of Ghiant. I've been doing a little amateur research into its history, you see."

Mrs Stewart pursed her lips, creating a fan of spidery lines around her mouth. "There's nothing to see on Ghiant any longer, Mr Hutchison. The last family left in the early sixties. My husband went there once, with the geographical survey team – back in '91. He says that the council haven't bothered to make the old buildings safe." She drained her mug. "It's certainly not a place for tourists."

Bill gripped his brush more tightly. "But there *are* ways of reaching it?"

She nodded begrudgingly. "You'd have to take the wee ferry boat to Nabb. I believe there's a chap at the harbour there who takes a speedboat over every so often to photograph the birds. He accommodates passengers for a fee. There may be other boats that go too."

Bill got to his feet. "Thank you, Mrs Stewart. I'll look into it."

Isla shook her head of cropped grey curls disapprovingly. "I hope you'll not be taking Mrs Hutchison with you on that trip. I'm not sure the territory will be suitable for a lady of her age - if you don't mind me saying."

"I don't mind at all, but I'm afraid that Joy is just as interested in the place as I am – even more so, perhaps."

Isla frowned, realising there wasn't going to be anything she could say to put the man off his scheme. She knelt down to retrieve Bill's mug, which was still half full and proceeded towards the sink, where she unceremoniously tipped the remainder down the drain, thinking that this couple who she'd found rather sweet and charming when they arrived, had turned out to be really quite odd.

*

The forecast had proved correct. Their sailing to the Isle of Nabb was comfortably smooth. The skipper, who Bill decided must be one of the Robertson brothers, brought the small vessel up to the jetty at Nabb harbour. Another man, with short sleeves and muscles that strained beneath them, pulled the boat into its mooring fiercely before securing the bow rope.

The stronger built of the two reached out a hand to each of the passengers on board and practically lifted them ashore. He took care to be gentle with Joy, who, despite her bulky walking gear, was beginning to look a little frail. With his wife safely escorted to the harbour wall, Bill raised his gaze to take in the scene.

The Isle of Nabb was only marginally larger than Rum. Its low-lying, undulating topography, largely laid to pasture, meant that the island possessed three decently sized settlements and enough farmland to support the economy. The harbour was located in the main village of Gordon. There was no impressive Cuillin peak to provide a backdrop to this small collection of shops and houses, as there was on its neighbouring Rum, but the landscape of the isle had its own, uniquely barren charm.

Bill had never visited Nabb before, but he had an immediate sense that the scene unfolding before them at the harbour was an unusual one. The Robertson brothers had been swept into a tight group of fellow sailors; their rugged faces even more deeply etched with lines than normal.

Joy slipped her arm through his. "Do we have to wait long for the boat over to Ghiant?" She asked innocently.

Bill frowned. "There should be a service running at midday." He took a few steps towards the cabal of burly men, just as one of them began gravely punching numbers into his mobile phone. "Excuse me," Bill called out to the Skipper who'd brought them over from Skye. "Where should we go to board the ferry for Ghiant?"

The eldest Robertson brother grimaced. "It won't be running today, I'm afraid. You and your wife will have to stay here in Gordon until I take the boat back to Armadale at five."

Bill couldn't hide his disappointment. "But the weather is perfect. I can't envisage any reason why the voyage to Ghiant wouldn't be possible."

Another man stepped out of the group, the one who'd just made the phone call. "It's nothin' to do wi' the conditions, Grandad. I've just been onto the polis at Portree."

Bill became suddenly alert.

"I took a group of zoology students out to Ghiant this morning. It seems they discovered more than they bargained for."

Nervous laughter rippled round the group.

"What did they find?" Bill asked flatly.

"A dead body," the man replied with relish. "Stripped to the bone by rats, but still clear to any observer it was human."

The younger Robertson rounded on the man sharply. "I don't know why you're enjoying this so much, Jim. These boats are our livelihood. Who's going to want to come to the Small Isles after *this*?"

The other man gave an unpleasant smirk, revealing a line of overlapping and misshapen teeth. "Oh, I think you'll find it's quite the reverse." He rubbed his weather-worn hands together with undisguised glee. "Give it a few hours and this harbour will be crawling wi' folk. We'll discover we've never been so busy in our whole lives."

Bill sighed deeply, deciding with sadness the man was probably quite right.

Chapter 2

The room seemed familiar to DCI Dani Bevan. She'd never been to the Isle of Nabb before, but the childhood she spent on the Inner Hebridean island of Colonsay, where her father was the primary school headmaster, meant the detective had often been in places just like The Gordon Hotel.

The bed was neatly made with a floral duvet set and positioned in the centre of the room, beneath a window which provided a view of Gordon's pretty bay. The harbour was just visible at the headland to the east.

Dani had her laptop and case files laid out on the bed. They'd arrived late the previous night, allowing themselves a few hours of shut-eye before making a start. There was no great urgency to begin the investigation. It wasn't Dani's case, or within the jurisdiction of her serious crime division. But the SIO had identified a link to Dani's past early on in his inquiries. He was intent upon exploiting it.

Stuffing her phone in a jacket pocket, Dani swung open the door before DS Andy Calder had time to knock on it.

"Morning, Ma'am. Hope you slept well."

Dani noticed her DS was sporting a wide grin. She supposed this was a pleasant change for him. They were out of Glasgow and working on a case which wasn't directly their responsibility.

DI Alice Mann looked less cheerful. "I hope there'll be time for me to get up to speed, Ma'am. I didn't get a chance to read anything on the ferry."

Andy mimed sticking a finger down his throat, before treating them to his best retching noises.

Alice elbowed him sharply. "The sea was bloody rough."

Dani looked at her pretty, freckled face, deciding she was even paler than usual. "I hope you're not coming down with anything, Alice. We could have asked Sharon to come instead."

"No, not at all," the DI replied swiftly. "I'm fighting fit."

"Alice could be suffering from the bubonic plague and she'd still be fitter than Sharon."

Dani shot Andy a stern look. "It's that kind of comment that lands male officers in deep shit with the disciplinary board."

Andy shrugged his broad shoulders dismissively. "It's the sort of thing I'd say to Sharon herself – it's affectionate."

Dani grunted, deciding this was a battle worth saving for another day. "We'll grab some breakfast in the dining room. Then I can fill you in on what we know so far, Alice."

*

Andy busied himself scraping the locally produced jam across his toast.

"The body was found in a barn on the outskirts of what was once the main village on Ghiant."

"But nobody lives there now?" Alice glanced at her boss over her coffee cup.

Dani shook her head. "Nope. The last inhabitants left in 1962. There just wasn't a way of making a living on the island any longer."

"It's not an unusual story," Andy added. "I read there are nearly 800 islands off the Scottish coast, plenty of them are deserted."

"That's true," Dani said. "But not all of them are used as a dumping ground for dead bodies."

"Not that we know of," Andy put in.

Dani shrugged off this unpleasant thought. "Anyway, there was significant degradation to the corpse due to rodents having fed on it for several days."

Andy glanced at the thickly spread strawberry jam on his triangle of toast, dropping it back on the plate. "We've got a time of death then?"

"The corpse was relatively fresh," Dani continued. "The *PM* suggested it had been on the island for 2-3 days. The murder site was somewhere else, however."

Alice raised her eyebrows quizzically.

"The cause of death was multiple stab wounds to the upper torso. There wasn't enough blood on the concrete floor of the barn for the murder to have been committed there."

"So, the island is definitely a dump site." Andy sipped his tea, having given up on the idea of food.

"Correct."

"And the identification of the body is the reason we're here?" Alice asked with trepidation.

Dani sighed. "Forensics are still running the DNA tests, but the dental records were conclusive. Plus, the glaring fact the body was clothed, with a purse containing cards with her ID on it."

"That could have been the killer throwing us off the scent. It wouldn't mean much without the forensic tests to back it up," Andy supplied.

"Well, it wasn't. We've definitely got a perp who doesn't care if his victim gets identified."

"Unless they didn't expect the body to ever be found," Alice suggested.

Dani crinkled her brow. "Whoever put her there made a rudimentary attempt to cover the body with straw. We've got to assume the killer had some local knowledge, otherwise they wouldn't have known Ghiant was uninhabited. They also must have been aware she'd be found at some point. Ghiant is quite a hot spot for naturalists. If the body had been buried, it might have been a different story."

"We definitely know the victim was a woman?" To Andy's irritation, Alice had begun taking notes.

Dani nodded. "The *PM* told us the woman was 5'9" tall, well-nourished and healthy. The ID and dental records informed us she was Juliet Lowther, a 48 year-old fitness instructor from Fort William."

"How on earth did she wind up dead on a deserted island out in the north Atlantic?" Alice puffed out her cheeks.

Dani cradled her cup in her hands. "Juliet wasn't always a fitness instructor. Up until five years ago she was a cop. In fact, she was a DI down at the Cowcaddens Road station back when I was a DC. We worked on a number of cases together. I suppose you could call her a mentor of mine." The DCI paused, taking a sip of her drink. "And a friend."

Alice nodded with understanding. "And that's why we're here."

Chapter 3

There wasn't a police station on Nabb. The nearest was at Portree on Skye. Detective Inspector Grant Peyton from the Highlands and Islands division, had brought a handful of officers over from the mainland and set up a temporary headquarters in the Nabb town hall.

Peyton was tall and wiry. His hair had receded back to his pate but was shaved short to his scalp to reduce the effect. Dani decided he was about her age. The DCI always found the H and I officers to be more laid back and less obviously ambitious than their city counterparts.

Tables had been spaced out around the hall. A number of locals were being interviewed at each of them. Peyton strode towards Dani as they surveyed the scene.

"DCI Bevan? Thank you so much for coming all this way to help, Ma'am. It's much appreciated." His handshake was as effusive as his words.

"This is my team – DI Alice Mann and DS Andy Calder."

DI Peyton nodded his recognition.

Dani gestured towards the tables. "I see you're busy already."

"I wanted to interview the locals as quickly as I could. Someone must have seen our killer taking a boat over to Ghiant – rented him a tender, perhaps. We've already lost nearly a week. Memories will start to fade."

Dani was impressed. "Is there anywhere else the perp could have sailed from to reach the dump site?"

Peyton led them towards a small office he was clearly using as his own. A map of the area was laid out on the desk. "According to the locals, Nabb and Ghiant were always twin islands, due to their close proximity and the relative calmness of the stretch of water between them."

"I can see that," Dani commented.

"It's possible to reach Ghiant direct from Rum or Armadale on Skye, but the crossing would be long and much rougher." The man rubbed his tall forehead. "I just don't see a person smuggling a dead body in a boat using one of the busier harbours to set off from. It makes more sense they'd take the shortest possible route, a place with fewer prying eyes. Which means that for now, Nabb has got to be our focus."

Andy nodded. "Does that mean you also believe the murder site is here on the island too, sir?"

Dani was glad her DS was being respectful. She was already impressed with the DI's operation.

Peyton wrinkled his brow. "It's surely not easy to cart a dead body around the place. Our victim was tall and well built. She had strong muscles and must have weighed over ten stone before the rats got to her. I can't believe the place of death was too far from where the boat set sail. The pathologist was quite confident that death had occurred only a few hours before the wildlife got to her, a day or two at the outside."

"Which means we can probably mark a circle on this map," Dani supplied, "showing a maximum search area for the murder site to be located. We've got some software that can do the job in minutes."

"Excellent," Peyton exclaimed. "This was just the kind of input I was hoping you could provide." He looked sheepish. "I don't suppose one of your team could assist my boys with that?"

Alice stepped forward. "I'll get the software set up right now."

Alice was busy showing one of the DCs how to use the geographic profiling software whilst Andy offered to help perform some of the interviews of local fishermen.

As soon as her team were out of earshot, DI Peyton caught Dani's arm. "I was hoping we might be able to go and grab a coffee somewhere and have a talk?"

Dani knew better than to be flattered by his keenness to get her alone. "Of course. I know you want to ask me about Juliet. It's why I'm here."

Peyton already seemed to have sussed out a good location for their interview. Or perhaps he had a knowledge of the island from previous visits. Dani didn't know the man well enough yet to make a judgement.

The lounge bar of the hotel by the harbour was empty but for the two police officers. A waitress brought them a tray of morning coffee.

Peyton tucked his long legs under the armchair and leant on the plunger of their cafétiere. "The DNA results are back. We're just waiting to locate a next of kin, although the dental records are conclusive enough." He glanced up. "You couldn't help us with that, could you?"

"Juliet didn't mention her family much. Her mother was living near Glasgow. I've no idea if she's still alive."

Peyton grimaced. "The mother has passed away. There was no evidence Juliet had ever given birth, so no kids."

Dani dredged her memory. "Was there an older brother? I seem to recall Juliet mentioning him once, but she wasn't in regular contact."

Peyton nodded. "Charles Lowther. We're still trying to track him down. Seems like he's our only surviving family member. He's worked abroad for most of his adult life."

"I'm surprised Juliet never married," Dani stirred cream into her coffee. "She left the force in her early forties. There was still time for her to make a life for herself."

"Suggesting you can't have a life whilst you are on the force?" Peyton said this without recrimination.

Dani smiled. "Well, can you?"

Peyton chuckled. "Probably not."

Dani noticed his wedding ring for the first time. It looked well-worn. She hoped the DI was the exception to the rule. "Juliet was completely dedicated to the job. When I worked with her, she never seemed to leave the station. She often told me it was the only way to get ahead as a woman in the force. You had to work twice as hard as the men."

"She was a good police officer?"

"Juliet was a DI by her late thirties, which was pretty impressive a decade ago. I found her meticulous as an SIO. She taught me a great deal about investigative procedure. Without her mentoring, I may not have risen through the ranks myself."

"But she took early retirement at 42. She'd not attempted to rise any higher herself?"

Dani sighed. "One of the cases we worked on had a profound effect on Juliet. It shook her faith in the institution."

Peyton remained silent, re-filling both their cups. This was the kind of information he'd set up this meeting to hear.

"Do you recall the bomb at Royston Road Bus Station in 2006?"

Peyton nodded, his expression grave.

"Of course, you would. It was the worst atrocity in Glasgow since the bombing of the Clyde in World War Two." Dani played with her cup. "I was on leave when it happened, back on Colonsay with my father. Juliet and the team at Cowcaddens were amongst the first on the scene of the blast. The station was less than a mile away. Twenty people were killed and dozens injured. You can imagine what it must have been like for those first responders."

"Aye, it's the kind of event we train for but hope to Christ never happens. It's incredibly rare in Scotland." He frowned deeply. "You said the case rocked her faith in the force. I can see how the bombing would have traumatised the officers involved, but my recollection is that the police responded in an exemplary fashion. Bravery awards were given out."

"Yes, Juliet received one herself for bringing out the walking wounded before the second bomb was defused." Dani thirstily sipped her sweet coffee, as if she herself were suffering from the shock. "But the incident changed her. We worked together for the next couple of years. There was a hardness and a cynicism that pervaded her team on those last few cases. The change in Juliet's character seemed to have infected us all."

Peyton sat back and folded his arms across his chest. "Did this change in character cause her to offend someone to the degree that they'd set out to brutally kill her?"

Dani sighed deeply. "Not that I'm aware of. Juliet departed from the Glasgow police force with little fanfare, but I honestly don't believe she left any enemies behind her. A handful of us were even still her friends."

Chapter 4

The island seemed to have emptied of visitors overnight. Bill Hutchison imagined it must have been because none of the wee ferry boats were permitted to perform their usual itinerary of excursions to the surrounding isles. Without these services, Nabb had little inherent appeal. Even the discovery of a body hadn't attracted the ghoul contingent just yet.

Joy had slipped her arm through her husband's as they strolled along the main street in Gordon. "It's a terrible disappointment that we can't get to Ghiant. It's a trip I've long imagined taking again."

"Aye, but the police need to be allowed to do their job. It should be a crime scene that can be kept largely preserved from human contamination."

Joy shivered under her fleece. "I keep picturing that woman, lying all alone in the barn. No one would have heard her cries for help."

Bill turned to catch her eye. "From what the boatman told us, the woman was most likely dead before her body reached Ghiant. You can remove that morbid image from your mind straight away."

Joy sighed with some relief. They paused to watch a group of local children hanging around on the pebbly beach, kicking the stones like they were dribbling a football.

"I recall my cousin Aisling talking about the primary school on Nabb. By the time she and little Rory were five, there was no school left on Ghiant. In fact, there were only a handful of families left living on the island at all by the mid-fifties. The weans had to travel each day on the rowing boat with my uncle to get an education of any kind."

"You can see why they finally made the decision to leave. It's amazing they stayed for so long."

"It was their home," Joy replied simply. "My mother and I only visited once. She wanted to see the life her sister had made for herself on this remote island with a man she'd only met a few times during the war."

"Did your aunt have any idea what his background was, when they first fell in love?"

"Not really. It was only once they'd returned to Ghiant that Catrin realised her new husband was the heir to a farm providing for a dwindling population, on a tiny island without even a proper ferry service."

"Was your aunt happy there?"

"Oh yes. The island was like a playground for Aisling and Rory. Apart from Rob's tractor and the post van, there were no cars to worry about. I recall an idyllic summer enjoyed at the farmhouse. I helped feed the animals in the morning and spent the long afternoons swimming off the flat, sandy beaches. It was heaven. I believe my mother thought so too. I remember her stifling tears when the time came to leave. I made no similar attempt to maintain composure. Mine flowed freely."

"You must surely have both missed your father? You'd been away for months." Bill furrowed his brow, obviously in sympathy with his father-in-law, now long dead.

Joy shrugged. "Dad worked long hours. I don't recall him noticing our presence much when he was at home. Mum cooked and cleaned for him, but there was little affection."

Bill cleared his throat. "I didn't realise that about them."

Joy's face broke into a wistful smile. "Not like Uncle Rob. He used to jump down from the tractor at the end of the day and scoop his children up into his arms – me too when I was there. I suppose they didn't have the stresses and strains we had on the mainland. They could be more demonstrative."

Bill wondered if this memory had become embellished with the passage of time. He imagined that the job of keeping a farm going in a remote and exposed landscape was a tough existence. The family had been forced to go in the end, when they could no longer afford to feed the animals.

Joy looked past the children to the distant contours of the hills on Skye. "When Rob got the offer of a job on Arisaig, from an old army mate, it led to much soul searching. He and Catrin had no choice in the end. The children needed to come first. They knew that the island would be left abandoned without them, but my mother said they always firmly believed it would become populated again. The land was fertile and many immigrants were coming to Britain in the 50s and 60s from the old colonies. Catrin was convinced that Ghiant would come to life once more."

"But it never did," Bill commented sadly. "Those migrants settled in the cities, where there were jobs and established communities."

Joy wiped a tear away with her sleeve. "Talking about the place has brought back so many memories. It feels devastating to think that our magical island has been reduced to a dumping ground for murderers."

Bill placed a protective arm around his wife's shoulders. He pulled her tightly to him and wondered if their coming here hadn't been a terrible mistake.

*

Andy Calder zipped up his jacket against the strong breeze whipping along the harbour wall. He was waiting for one of the fishing boats to come back in. There was a man on board that the Highlands and Islands' team had yet to interview.

The DS glanced around the quiet port, allowing his gaze to run along the stretch of pastel-fronted houses that lay to the far side of the bay. His vision stopped abruptly at the outline of an old couple standing at the top of the beach, beyond a group of kids messing about on the stones. He shook his head as if to correct the image he was seeing. When he squinted into the distance again, the pair had gone.

"It couldn't possibly have been," he muttered to himself, turning back towards the sea, where a small boat was fighting the swell, motoring in his direction.

A bulky man, wearing a cable-knit sweater under his life jacket, leapt onto the jetty, securing the rope to its mooring.

Andy approached him, holding up his warrant card. "Can I have five minutes of your time, sir?"

The man dipped his head towards the boat. "We've got a catch to unload."

"Are you Sean Ballater?" Andy stood his ground.

"Aye, this is my boat, the Lady of Kinloch."

"My colleagues have experienced some difficulties getting hold of you, Mr Ballater. We're running a murder investigation here on Nabb. If I can't get a formal interview from you, I'm afraid you're looking at a charge of obstruction."

Ballater's blue eyes narrowed. "I suppose my crew can bring the catch in themselves." He turned and gestured towards one of the men lugging crates into piles on the gunwales before following Calder towards the stone building which housed the harbour master's office.

Andy took a seat behind a large, messy desk. Ballater rested his weight on a trestle table by the door. The man looked exhausted. Dark rings encircled his eyes, which were hooded and watchful.

"You'll be aware that a body was discovered at Rushbrooke Farm on Ghiant two days ago. Jim Lyle made the discovery and phoned the police. In his interview, he mentioned your name. Lyle told us you often made trips to the island."

Ballater nodded. "I wasn't the only fisherman who did. I occasionally laid some pots around the bay. I decided there might be rich pickings with nobody living out there. In reality, I reckon the wildlife's taken over. The otters get most of it."

"When was the last time you sailed out to Ghiant?"

Ballater shifted his weight uncomfortably. "It was last Thursday. I had a couple of pots to check."

Andy made a note and glanced up. "Did you take the Lady of Kinloch?"

The fisherman sneered. "Of course not. I took out my tender. It's got a small outboard motor."

"We'll need to take a look at it," Andy replied.

He shrugged. "If you must. I keep it at home. We live a few miles north of here."

"And did you see anything unusual during this visit to Ghiant?"

"Like a woman being murdered, you mean?" Ballater responded, his tone dripping with sarcasm.

Andy kept his cool. Sitting upright and spreading his hands out on the desk, he continued. "Any other boats moored up, signs of the vegetation having been disturbed, that kind of thing. There can't be many folks who go out there regularly. Anything you noticed could be significant." The DS fixed his glare on the man opposite. "Unless of course, the killer is one of you fisherman – You, Lyle or the Robertson brothers. You've all got the access required to dump a body there and the knowledge of the landscape.

You're also fit enough to haul a corpse about. There aren't many others I've interviewed who fit that bill."

Ballater got to his feet.

For a moment, Andy thought he was about to storm out. Then the man stepped forward and dropped into a chair, resting his head in both hands. "I'm sorry I've been evasive. I've been out skippering the boat for long hours recently. The last few nights I've barely slept. That's why I missed your colleagues when they called round. I'm dog tired." He raised his head. "I'm trying to make extra cash right now. My missus is expecting. The bairn's due in the Autumn."

Andy was taken aback by the man's abrupt change in mood. "Congratulations," he said dryly. "But a woman's been killed, Mr Ballater. We need your cooperation."

He nodded. "Aye. But there's really nothing to tell. Ghiant was the same as always when I went there the other day. The buildings are half falling down. I doubt if anyone would really notice there'd been trespassers. Occasionally, I see the remains of a camp fire on the beach – usually in summer. But not this time. The weather's not been good enough for that."

Andy leaned forward. "So, the place does get visitors, other than just the twitchers and tree-hugging types?"

Ballater's postured stiffened just a fraction. "Not regularly. But kids with a rowing boat might head out there on a calm evening – take some tins of beer and a few packets of smokes – away from their parents, you know? The island could be a place for the youngsters of Nabb and Rum to do the stuff their folks wouldn't approve of, away from prying eyes."

"It sounds as if you're talking from experience?" Andy raised an eyebrow.

Ballater's drawn face finally cracked a grin. "I'm

too old for that kinda thing now, Sergeant." He winked, but then his cheerful expression fell, as if realisation had suddenly dawned. "And I've got far too many bloody responsibilities."

Chapter 5

The interview transcripts that Andy had supplied Dani with weren't throwing up any decent leads. DI Peyton was sending a couple of men out to examine Sean Ballater's boat, but their searches so far hadn't indicated any connection between the fisherman and Juliet Lowther.

Dani was certain they needed to concentrate more on the victim. It was where her murder investigations always started.

The DCI carried her laptop down to the sitting room of the Gordon Hotel. The room had a pleasant view of the bay which was currently obscured by low-lying cloud. She closed her eyes for a moment, trying to recall the Juliet she had known back in Glasgow. It was difficult to shift the image of her old friend now imprinted upon her mind's eye by the clinical brutality of the crime scene photographs.

But after a while, Dani managed to re-capture a picture of Lowther as a young DI, leaning across her desk and drawing in her team with those piercing, sky blue eyes.

One of the earliest cases they worked on together involved the suspicious death of a minor at a rehabilitation centre for recovering addicts in Sighthill. The publicity hadn't been welcomed by the local authority who ran the facility. But Juliet had been determined to investigate the young man's death thoroughly.

Dani sipped the coffee she'd ordered and tried to summon up the details of that particular case. The boy who died was fifteen years old, although she couldn't recall his name. His body was found in the gymnasium early one morning. He had a nasty head wound and bruising to his back and shins. The staff claimed he'd been using the equipment after hours and fell to the hard floor where he passed away from his injuries.

The *PM* was inconclusive, but revealed traces of alcohol and marijuana in his system. This triggered a full investigation. The boys at the centre shouldn't have been able to get hold of any drugs.

Dani recalled how tenacious Juliet had been in her questioning. They liaised regularly with the boy's parents who were devastated. They'd had him committed to the facility to get him cured, not to sign his death warrant.

What they discovered was a web of corruption amongst the staff, who took money in return for distributing small amounts of weed and bottles of booze amongst the patients. The boy's death was deemed unlawful due to a breach of care by the institution and the local authority. The parents received a moderate pay-out and the centre was closed down.

Dani wondered if Juliet had made any enemies during that case. A couple of dozen people lost their jobs and a handful were convicted of minor drug offenses. No single individual was blamed for the boy's death. As far as Dani was concerned, the employees at the centre got off lightly. The governor even went on to manage other facilities, claiming he knew nothing about the illegal actions of his staff.

There didn't appear to be any reason why this investigation would be connected to Juliet's murder. Dani sighed, lifting her cup to her lips and draining the contents. She stared hard at the curtain of wispy clouds hanging over the water, as if they represented the fug that seemed to be enveloping her brain. It was preventing her from extracting with any clarity the memories of her time at Cowcaddens Road Police Station which were necessary to provide Peyton with the information he wanted. If she looked closely enough, perhaps the mist would clear.

"Aye, the weather could certainly be better," a voice behind Dani abruptly declared. She'd been so engrossed in her own thoughts that she'd not noticed anyone else entering the room.

The DCI twisted around to face the person who had interrupted her reverie. "*Bill?* What on earth are *you* doing here?"

Bill Hutchison pulled up a chair and joined her. "I might ask you the same thing. Joy and I are on holiday. We were hoping to do some island hopping, then the boatman made a grisly discovery and put our plans on hold. We're staying at a B&B on the other side of the bay."

Dani shook her head vigorously, in undisguised disbelief. "I had no idea you were on Nabb. Have you been interviewed by the Highlands and Islands detectives?"

"Aye, on the day the body was found. Joy and I were at the harbour when the police were called. We gave a brief statement, but the officers weren't much interested in what we had to say. We'd only just arrived, you see. We'd not set foot on Ghiant yet."

Dani glanced down at the file placed on the table between them. "I hadn't got around to reading all of the statements yet."

"Well. You'll not find anything useful in ours."

She took a deep breath, trying to regain some composure. "How is Joy – are you both keeping well?" Dani felt a sudden pang of guilt, that since a mutual friend of theirs had been killed the year before, she'd barely spoken to the couple, when they'd once been quite close. It had proved a case of 'out of sight, out of mind', she supposed.

"Joy has become a little frail in the past six months, I can't deny. She took Sergeant Sharpe's death rather badly. We were both very fond of him."

Dani leant forward and placed her hand on his arm. "I'm sorry I haven't really been in touch since the funeral. I didn't find Sam's death easy either. It seemed simpler to focus on my work."

Bill nodded sagely. "But you can't push away everyone who reminds you of him. The grief will catch up with you in the end."

Dani cleared her throat. This wasn't a conversation she was keen to have right now. "Why are you and Joy still here? There's not much to see on Nabb. The ferry is running to Armadale. I would suggest you opt for a different route. Skye is very beautiful at this time of year."

Bill nodded. "I know it seems odd that we're hanging about like this, but there's more to it than a thwarted day trip." He raised his gaze to meet hers. "Joy's aunt and her family lived on Ghiant in the forties and fifties. They were amongst the last inhabitants to leave the island. She has wanted to go back and see the place for decades. This was the first time we'd got around to making the arrangements. If I'm honest, I was worried that in future years, Joy might not still be able to manage the trip."

Dani shuffled forward in her seat, her interest piqued. "So, Joy has a connection to the island? Did you mention this to the officers who interviewed you?"

Bill shook his head. "It didn't seem relevant. The detective simply wanted the details of our movements in the last few days."

"Yes, that would be normal procedure." She ran a hand through her hair. "But we're struggling to find a reason why the victim was left on the island. This case is anything but normal. In this instance, I think it would be worth us finding out everything there is to know about the abandoned Isle of Ghiant. Joy may be just the person to help us."

A flash of excitement showed in Bill's eyes. "Well, if you really believe it would be of use to the investigation, Joy and I would be pleased to offer our assistance."

Chapter 6

Grant Peyton had called a briefing. The detectives gathered in the town hall, beneath a stage area with polished wooden boards upon which the DI had erected a flip chart.

"First of all," the man began. "I'd like to thank Alice for her assistance with the geographic profiling software. It has allowed us to produce this map."

Peyton pinned a print-out to the chart. It showed a map of Skye and the Small Isles, encompassing parts of the mainland and reaching as far west as South Uist. "The red circle indicates the area in which our murder site is most likely located."

Dani examined the locations carefully. She grimaced. "Juliet might have been killed on the mainland. That's going to make our job much harder."

"Yes, but the parameters of the circle don't reach as far as her home in Fort William. Perhaps she travelled out to the west coast of her own volition," Peyton suggested. "In which case, there may be a record somewhere of her trip."

"Or the perp kidnapped her from her home and brought her to the murder site in the boot of a car or the back of a van," Andy chipped in.

Peyton shook his head. "We've had a forensic team at the victim's flat. There was no sign there that indicated an abduction. The bed was recently slept in by the victim and carefully made. All the prints we identified on the premises were Ms Lowther's. Any others were purely historic. She clearly didn't have many visitors."

"Did you remove any personal items – like a computer or written correspondence?" Dani was suddenly alert.

Peyton nodded. "The team at Fort William are analysing the personal contents they found at the place. There was no mobile phone on Juliet's body and none in her home. We're currently requesting her landline records."

"I'd like to take a look at anything you find," Dani said.

"Of course," he replied.

Alice shook her head of auburn hair. "Do we think the perp dumped the victim's mobile phone before leaving the body on Ghiant? It seems strange to go to the effort of doing that whilst leaving a purse full of identification cards on her person."

"It may seem impossible for someone of your age to comprehend," Peyton added with a wry grin, "but perhaps the woman didn't actually own a mobile."

Dani nodded slowly. "Juliet certainly didn't possess a personal mobile phone when I knew her, only one issued by the Force. However, that was a long time ago. But I agree with DI Peyton, it seems entirely possible to me that Juliet didn't have her own phone. She was always a private person, with few friends or family."

"We'll check her standing orders and make sure," Peyton added.

"She could have had a pay-as-you-go," Andy muttered, almost under his breath. Like Alice, he wasn't convinced that anyone in this day and age wouldn't have a mobile phone, let alone an ex-cop. More loudly, he announced, "what about Sean Ballater's boat? Did the examination bring up anything of interest?"

One of the Highlands and Islands officers stepped

forward. "When we arrived at the address you gave us, which is along a dirt track about two miles from here, only Mrs Ballater was at home. She allowed us full access to the shed where her husband keeps his boats and fishing gear. We went through the lot." He swept a hand through his coarse, tightly curled hair. "The tender had clearly been out recently. There was still seawater in the hull. The thing was fairly battered up, with no signs it had been recently cleaned. There were lobster pots tied all around the inside, with ancient rust adhered to the ropes securing them there. I cannae see how Ballater could have used it to shift a body as recently as a few days back. Those older pots hadn't been shifted in years. There just wouldn't have been room enough."

Dani was impressed by the thoroughness of the officer's observations. "What did the wife have to say about her husband's movements?"

The officer shrugged his shoulders. "She certainly didn't attempt to provide him with an alibi. Apparently, Ballater is out on the water most days and doesn't come home until late."

"That's the same thing he told me," Andy confirmed.

"Well, the Ballater place certainly isn't our murder site," the officer added.

"Okay," Peyton said with a certain disappointment in his tone. "We need to get back to finding out where is. I'm certain the key will be in locating the boat that took the body out to Ghiant. I've got officers asking questions at all the ports and harbours within our search area. The Fiscal has provided a warrant to search any vessels they have suspicions about."

Dani nodded encouragingly. "Good." Then the DCI shifted from one foot to the other, clearing her throat awkwardly.

"Was there something else, Ma'am?" Peyton enquired.

"Actually, there was. It may not be significant, but a couple of friends of mine are here on Nabb. They were at the harbour when the fishermen who found the body were first questioned."

Peyton raised his head with a jerk, suddenly alert. "Did these friends know Juliet Lowther too?"

Dani shook her head vigorously. "No, not at all. It's just that one of them had relatives on Ghiant when it was still inhabited. It was why they were trying to travel out there. I thought it might be worth questioning her more thoroughly about the place. Perhaps the island was chosen as a dumping site for a reason."

The DI shrugged his shoulders. "Maybe so. We aren't exactly swamped with leads, so it's worth a punt." Peyton gestured to one of his officers. "Tom, would you mind taking down the name and looking into it?"

Dani turned to the young officer. "Her name is Joyce Hutchison. The couple are staying at the Celtic Thistle B&B."

Andy let out what sounded like a cross between a cough and a laugh. "The *Hutchisons* are here?" He slapped his knee. "I could've sworn I saw them the other day by the shore, but I persuaded myself it was simply my mind playing tricks."

"Oh, they're here all right," Dani added grimly. "Slap bang in the middle of our murder investigation."

Chapter 7

"Of course, I haven't been up the Cuillin Ridge since I was a young man. If you're lucky enough to have a day when the mist isn't down, the views are truly spectacular."

DC Tom Carrick had left his pen poised over his pad for the last twenty minutes. He was struggling to decipher what was relevant to their investigation from the good-natured ramblings of this old couple.

Bill Hutchison stood and approached the bar to order another pot of tea from one of the hospitality team dressed in a smart tartan skirt and jacket.

Tom seized his moment to address a question to Joy. "Mrs Hutchison, the DCI told me that you'd once visited Ghiant when it was still a thriving island. That must have been something, eh?"

Joy nodded enthusiastically. "My aunty married a Rushbrooke. She had no idea when she met Rob during the war, that marrying him would mean taking on the Rushbrooke smallholding on Ghiant. It came as quite a surprise, I can tell you."

Tom was a little taken aback himself. This sweet little lady seated before him was probably the last living relative of the owners of Rushbrooke Farm, where Juliet Lowther's body had been dumped. "When was the farm last occupied?" He asked innocently.

"My family were amongst the last to be evacuated. The boats came in May 1962. Aunty Catrin packed as much as she could in suitcases and a few boxes. But that was all they could manage." Joy's expression became suddenly dreamy. "Most of the furniture and fittings were left behind. Much as if people were still living there. My cousin went back a few years later and it made her cry to see the place as if it were stuck in time. Nature had taken over on the ground floors, but her old bedroom was much as she'd left it. The strong winds rattling through the decaying building hadn't even allowed the dust to settle."

Bill was back at the table, watching his wife carefully, sensing it was time to let her speak.

"There was a small package of government compensation, which allowed Catrin and Rob to set up in a cottage in Arisaig, where an old army friend of Rob's gave him a job."

"It doesn't seem much of a replacement when you've lost your family business and the home of your forebears," Tom added with genuine feeling.

"Oh, the islanders were used to such injustices," Bill chipped in. "The forcible evictions during the highland clearances of the mid-nineteenth century had already ravaged many island communities and left hard-working folk with nothing."

Concerned that the old man might be about to launch into a lengthy history of the western isles, Tom quickly said, "Joy, can you recall any of the other families who lived on Ghiant with the Rushbrookes?"

Joy furrowed her brow and sipped some tea. "There was a family living near the farm who ran the post office and store. They were amongst the last to leave along with Catrin and Rob." She shook her head in frustration. "I simply cannot recall their names. I know we played with the post master's boy, who was the same age as myself and Aisling. There were a few others, in the crofters' cottages further up the hill. I'm sorry, I can't remember who any of them were."

Tom was worried the woman was about to cry. Tears had pooled in her eyes, dislodging the clumpy mascara edging them. "Not to worry, madam. It was over fifty years ago. Nobody would expect you to, it was a silly question."

"The memory of her family on Ghiant makes my wife upset sometimes," Bill said by way of explanation. "Joy and I have lost so much in the course of our lives. The abandoned island has become a symbol of this loss for us."

The policeman didn't entirely understand what Hutchison was on about, but he recognised that their interview was over. He finished off his tea. "Thank you very much for your assistance, Mrs Hutchison. You've been most helpful."

*

Dani had taken the morning ferry to Arisaig on the mainland, where local officers had supplied her with an unmarked car for the drive to Fort William.

The journey took less than an hour. The route was nothing less than stunning. The mighty Glenfinnan viaduct marked the halfway point and as she swept through the streets of Fort William, searching for her destination, the peak of Ben Nevis flashed in and out of view.

The block of flats was unremarkable by comparison. A tall man with a creased jacket leant against the wall by the entrance doors. He put out a hand as Dani approached.

"DS Forrest, Ma'am."

The DCI introduced herself. "Can we go inside?"

"Aye, and I've brought over the effects that you requested."

Juliet's flat was on the first floor. A tiny printed name tag had been slotted into a plastic casing above the bell. The DS produced a key ring and turned a deadlock before using the Yale.

"Not bad security," Dani commented.

"That's right. We found no evidence of a break-in. The windows were all secure. There's a buzzer entry system down on ground level too, but we know how easy they are to bypass."

"When did her neighbours last see Ms Lowther?" Dani was allowing her gaze to take in the compact arrangement of small rooms.

"The retired lady below saw her on the Saturday morning before her death. She happened to be out front pruning the rose bush. She said Juliet went out with a shopping bag about mid-morning and came home an hour later. She's seen nothing since, but says that's not unusual. Her sitting room window faces the garden rather than the street. That's where the old dear spends most of her time. It's a modern block with pretty good sound-proofing."

Dani noticed that a neat stack of papers had been placed on the narrow kitchen table. "Are those her effects?"

Forrest nodded. "Aye, sit down and have a read. I need to go and get myself a sandwich anyhow. There's a petrol garage at the end of the street. Want me to fetch you something, Ma'am?"

Dani glanced up. "Sure, I'll have anything edible that looks fresh, and a coffee, if there's a decent machine."

The DS seemed pleased, perhaps worrying that the DCI was a single-minded city-type who didn't approve of lunch breaks.

Dani wasn't actually that hungry, but she wanted to be left alone with Juliet's documents for as long as possible. From the residual smell of stale tobacco that clung to the officer's clothes, she assumed he'd also take the time to have a smoke while he was gone. It suited her fine.

When the door to the flat was pulled shut, Dani went straight into the bedroom, where it was always possible to gain a reasonable sense of the person who occupied it. The bed was a small double, pushed to one wall to accommodate an exercise bench with weights resting on it. A single wardrobe housed a rail of simple blouses and tailored trousers, the drawers beneath holding the well-worn sweatshirts and jogging pants which were clearly Juliet's usual attire.

There were no photographs on the bedside table or windowsill and the painted walls were devoid of ornamentation. The room was sterile and anonymous. It reminded Dani of a prison cell. The kind that those convicts lucky enough to be sent to one of Scotland's more modern institutions would be allocated.

She exited swiftly and sat on an uncomfortable stool to survey the paperwork. Highlands and Islands had made copies of everything. Amongst the copious sheets was a thick pile of bank statements. Juliet's main income was her police pension, which she supplemented with cheques from clients who used her services as a fitness instructor. The sums were modest, but then, so were the woman's outgoings. The rent and bills on the flat didn't make much of a dent and Juliet barely withdrew much else.

The former policewoman was living an almost ascetic existence here in Fort William. Dani tried to recall if this matched with what she knew of Juliet's character back in their days at Cowcaddens Road.

DI Lowther had worked hard, but then she'd

played hard too. The officers used to drink in Dobbie's Bar, not far from what was the old Glasgow Poly. Juliet enjoyed a whisky like many of her male counterparts. The DCI even recalled being given a lift by her mentor on one occasion. They'd attended a training class together on a Saturday morning. Dani had a vague recollection that Juliet's car was small but sporty, the seats covered in a luxurious leather.

Dani was the only one of her contemporaries who didn't drink heavily back in those days. The knowledge of what had happened to her mother prevented that. It made Dani something of an outsider, until she rose through the ranks and the culture within policing started to change.

But Juliet was of that old guard. Dani recalled the smoke-filled backroom of Dobbie's, where bottles of scotch lined up along the dark wooden tables between the officers and their chubby, expensive cigars, smouldering in ashtrays. In the mornings which followed one of these nights, Dani would wake to find her throat coated in an unpleasant, tar-like substance. The nasty deposit had to be vigorously coughed away, even though she'd not taken a single puff from one of the cigars herself.

The sound of the front door opening shook Dani abruptly out of the memory. But the smell of fresh cigarette smoke that followed DS Forrest into the flat transported the DCI straight back to the seedy pub nights of her early career.

She accepted her lunch with a grateful smile and returned to the task.

Chapter 8

The man who entered DI Peyton's tiny temporary office was tall and broad. He almost filled the entire space.

Grant shook his hand solemnly. "You didn't need to travel out here to Nabb, sir. Your sister's body has been taken to a mortuary on the mainland."

Charles Lowther nodded. "I know, but I wanted to come out here and see where Juliet was found." The man possessed a head of thick silver hair. A deep tan illuminated his rugged skin. His voice was tinged with a hint of transatlantic drawl.

"When did you last see you sister?" Peyton perched on the edge of a bookcase, aware of how dwarfed he would be if he sat at the desk chair.

Lowther rubbed his chin. "I'm ashamed to admit it was a couple of years ago. I came to Glasgow on a business trip in 2015, we met for dinner whilst I was there. Juliet never came out to LA to visit."

"Was there a reason for that? You were her only family, after all."

He crinkled his forehead into a frown. "I left the UK twenty-five years go. Juliet was a busy cop but still found the time to care for our mother in old age. I believe my sister felt I'd abdicated my responsibilities for the good life. We'd not been close since we were kids."

Peyton nodded. "Your mother died in 2013?"

"That's right. My wife and I flew over for the funeral, but we left the girls with Sasha's mom. My daughters had never really known their Grandma."

"So, you weren't in regular contact with Juliet in recent years – you have no knowledge of whether she had a boyfriend or if there were any issues that were troubling her?" Peyton scanned the man's face. His expression was frozen with tension. A blood vessel was pumping on his right temple.

"Juliet was a very resilient, independent woman. I don't reckon there was a man out there who would've been a match for her long-term." He sighed heavily. "If anything bad was going on with Juliet, I'd have been the last person she'd tell."

Peyton dipped his head. "Okay, that's enough questions for now. I've arranged for one of the police boats to take you out to Ghiant at eleven. Have you packed anything warm?"

"Sure. I haven't been away from Scotland for so long that I'm not prepared for the weather." His broad shoulders relaxed a little. "I just want to see where she was laid, Inspector. I'm hoping it will make me feel closer to her – less like I'd abandoned her completely."

The DI placed his hand on Lowther's arm. "I understand. She's at peace now."

He cleared his throat. "When can I start planning the funeral."

"The *PM* has been completed but this is still an ongoing murder investigation. It might be a few weeks before we release her to you."

Lowther nodded, obviously not trusting himself to speak. Tears were pooling in his eyes.

"I'm not sure how Juliet felt about the force in the last few years," Peyton continued, "but the DCC would like to give your sister a police funeral. She'd served with us valiantly for a long time. Juliet won several medals for bravery."

The tears finally escaped, running through the

rivulets of his coarsely lined cheeks. "I think she'd have wanted that. Our mom was so proud of her when she made DI. Far prouder than she'd ever been of me."

*

The stone causeway had suffered from the merciless erosion of the sea. Part of it had long since slumped under the waves and Charles Lowther had to wade through knee-deep water to come ashore from the police tender.

Peyton followed at a respectful distance. He allowed the man to reach the main road of Ghiant's largest settlement before he caught him up and directed Lowther towards what remained of Rushbrooke Farm.

The outhouse in which Juliet's body had been found was cordoned off with police tape. Peyton had made the decision not to assign one of his officers to preserve the scene. They'd got all the forensics they needed. An area so open to the elements would very quickly be of no use to them. The tape was only really still in place as a mark of respect. As it was, the local police were strictly limiting the number of vessels allowed access to the island.

The DI led the way to a far corner of the barn. The roof was entirely gone and the concrete floor was strewn with leaves and branches, except for the oblong area where the body had lain, which was newly cleared. Peyton was suddenly relieved that the wounds had bled out before the victim had reached this point. He wouldn't have wanted Charles to see the inevitable stains that would have remained otherwise.

Lowther got down on his haunches, glancing

about him. "How long was Juliet here before someone found her?"

"A day or two at the most," Peyton replied. "But she was already dead before reaching here. We are currently trying to find the place where she was assaulted."

Lowther turned his head and met the DI's gaze. "And the cause of death were the multiple stab wounds to the body?"

Peyton thought the man almost sounded like an expert. Then everyone was these days, with the benefit of wall-to-wall crime dramas on the telly. "Yes. Death would have been swift, particularly once the carotid artery was severed."

"There would have been a lot of blood, then?" Lowther's statement was almost clinical, delivered without emotion.

"That's correct. It's the reason we know Juliet wasn't killed here."

Lowther slowly stood. "The attack on Juliet must have been incredibly ferocious and violent. What did my sister do to invoke such fury and hatred?"

Peyton could tell the man was trying to make sense of the event. It happened all the time with families of victims of particularly brutal crimes. The sad thing was, there was often no satisfactory explanation. "We're trying to find that out, sir. From our investigations so far, Juliet appears to have been a loner since leaving the Force. In this type of assault, we usually look carefully at a lover or ex-lover. If the perpetrator were a spurned or jealous partner it would go some way to explain the passion involved in the manner of the crime."

"But Juliet didn't have a lover," Lowther commented. "Or not one she told anyone about."

"Was your sister a lesbian?" Peyton knew that plenty of his fellow female officers were. He thought it might explain why Juliet kept her love life private.

Lowther shook his head. "I really don't think so. Juliet had plenty of boyfriends as a teenager." He wrinkled his face in thought. "I'm sure she had a bloke when she was based in Glasgow. He was a fellow officer, I'm sure. I think I even met him at Mum's place once."

"How long ago was this?" Peyton tried to hide his excitement.

"It must be over a decade. I got the sense he was long off the scene now." Lowther looked about him and shuddered, as if abruptly realising where he was. "I think I want to leave this place now."

"Of course." Peyton led the way back to the jetty.

Clouds were moving in from the west, covering the sun and removing any hint of warmth.

The tide had dropped and the police skipper had brought the tender up onto the beach. Peyton climbed in first and offered his hand to Lowther.

As they gazed back at the darkening landscape, Peyton had a sudden thought. "Mr Lowther, had your sister been to this island before? Is it somewhere your family visited? We're working on the possibility that Juliet was brought here for a reason."

Lowther shook his head. "I can't see any reason why she'd come to a lonely place like this. I certainly don't recall our folks ever bringing us here." His thick body shuddered once again, despite the padded jacket he was wearing. "I mean, why the heck would you want to?"

Chapter 9

A fire had been lit in the grate. Alice and Andy sat opposite one another in leather high-backed chairs, tumblers of whisky resting on the arms.

"When is the boss due back from Fort William?" Alice asked.

Her companion shrugged. "She's still liaising with the officers examining the victim's property. After that, Bevan suggested she might return to Glasgow and talk to a few of Lowther's ex-colleagues at Cowcaddens."

The DI nodded. "So, we'll focus on helping Peyton find the murder scene?"

Andy finished his dram. "Aye, but it's a huge task. The brother turning up hasn't provided us with any fresh information as to why the victim would have been in this area before she died."

Alice sighed. "He'd barely seen his sister in two decades." She turned and signalled to the barman of the Gordon Hotel to bring them a couple more shots. "He didn't know Juliet at all."

"The woman was certainly a loner."

Alice relaxed back into the worn upholstery, cradling the whisky in her hands. "I hope I don't end up like that after I retire."

Andy chuckled. "It's hardly in prospect. You've got Fergus now anyway. It's more likely to be Dan or Sharon who'll be heading up the lonely hearts' club."

Alice grimaced. "Don't let them hear you say that. I expect they both believe there's plenty of time left for them to meet the right person. I certainly wasn't looking for a relationship when Fergus came along." She tipped her glass towards Andy. "You never know, Carol might finally get sick of you. Dan and Sharon might not be the only ones in that club come retirement."

Andy looked suddenly wistful. "Aye, you may well be right there. I don't really deserve her and Amy."

Alice cleared her throat awkwardly, she'd only meant the comment as a friendly jibe. Calder was quick to dish out the abuse, he couldn't be too sensitive about being on the receiving end. She changed the subject. "Are you still suspicious about that fisherman you interviewed? The forensics on his boat came back clear."

"He evaded interview for several days and spends a lot of time alone on Ghiant. He seemed to be suggesting that folk from the other islands used the place for illicit activities. I reckon Ballater has either witnessed this stuff or taken part in it himself. I'd like to have another word with him. Maybe you could come too, see what you make of the guy?"

"Sure, good idea."

Andy glanced past the wing-back of Alice's chair and watched an elderly couple exiting the dining room, arm-in-arm. He rose to his feet and waved them over. "Come and have a nightcap with us," he called out.

Bill and Joy turned their heads at the sound of Calder's voice. Bill glanced solicitously at his wife. "We'll join you for a quick one, Detective Sergeant, then it will be time for us to turn in."

Alice pulled across another couple of chairs. Andy ordered the brandies.

"It's good of you to remember our tipple," Bill commented amiably.

"We've been through our fair share of crises together," Andy said with a grin. "I could hardly forget."

Alice surreptitiously took in the appearance of Joy Hutchison, who seemed small and frail in the oversized chair. The woman didn't appear well. Which made her next comment deeply ironic.

"You look very pale, DI Mann. I hope you're not coming down with something. Perhaps you caught a chill on the ferry crossing?"

Alice rubbed at her cheeks, a subconscious practice she'd adopted for when she wanted to inject some colour into them. "I'm feeling grand, Mrs Hutchison. This case is less strenuous for us than most."

"Because DI Peyton is the SIO?" Bill suggested.

Andy nodded. "We're here to consult with Highlands and Islands. The buck stops with them."

"But once you're involved in a murder case, there must surely be the same desire to find the perpetrator, especially when you get to know the background of the victim?" Bill received two brandies from the waiter and set one down in front of Joy.

"Aye, that's true. And in this instance, the boss did actually know the victim. It's the reason we're here."

Bill narrowed his eyes with curiosity. "Oh yes?"

Andy lowered his voice. "The victim was a retired police officer. Dani had worked under her down in Glasgow, earlier in her career. The SIO wants the boss to help build a character profile of the victim."

Alice cast him a warning look. "We shouldn't discuss the details of the case," she muttered.

"It's okay. Bill and Joy have really helped us in the past," he added cheerfully. "Bill's provided some valuable input over the years. I'd even suggest his insights have cracked a couple of big cases."

Bill shook his head bashfully. "I wouldn't go that far, DS Calder."

Joy sipped her brandy, seeming to find it a struggle to swallow. Once she had, she glanced at Andy. "Did the DCI know this woman well? Is she very upset by the murder? Because Danielle has had enough on her plate in recent years."

Andy nodded. "I can understand your concern, but Dani hadn't been in contact with the woman for over ten years. The relationship revolved around the job."

"Still," Bill added, "the case has a personal dimension for Danielle. We hadn't realised that."

Alice suddenly got to her feet. "I'm tired after a long day. Please excuse me, I'm going up to my room." The DI opened her wallet and left a crisp note on the table, exiting the lounge with haste.

Joy turned to watch her depart. "That young lady isn't at all well."

"I hope it's nothing contagious," Andy added with a frown.

Bill leant forward conspiratorially. "I'm glad we've got you alone, DS Calder."

Andy drained his glass, experiencing an unpleasant tingle of apprehension. "Oh, aye?"

Bill took Joy's hand. "I know it must seem odd to you, us still being here on Nabb?"

Andy shrugged his shoulders. The Hutchisons had always been unconventional. This wasn't the weirdest thing they'd ever done.

"But you see, it has become very important that we remain close to the island."

Andy crinkled his brow, confused about Bill's meaning.

"Ghiant. The island where Joy's family lived." The older man smoothed down his corduroy trousers, before lifting his gaze to meet Andy's again. "The island has great significance for Joy. She's waited a long time to return there. It represents an intensely happy time from her past."

Andy was starting to feel uncomfortable about where this was going.

Bill cast his wife a sideward glance and clutched her hand more tightly. "We've suffered great loss in our lives. The passing of Sergeant Sharpe, the man who saved my life, was yet another such tragedy." He cleared his throat. "Since then, Joy has been having the most vivid dreams about Ghiant. Her memories of the place are crystal-clear. We have grown certain over recent months that we must go there. Joy's health is deteriorating. We haven't much time. I *know* that the island will heal her."

Andy had already begun shaking his head sadly.

Bill put up his hand. "I realise the island is now under the jurisdiction of the police. But there must be special circumstances in which a visit could be permitted?"

"The SIO would never agree to it. Peyton has ordered that no tourist boats land for the foreseeable future, certainly not until the murder is solved. He doesn't know you both. Added to that, you were here when the body was found. To all intents and purposes, you are potential suspects."

Bill glanced around furtively, as if double-checking they were alone in the deserted lounge bar. "Then, does the man have to know about it? All we need is access to a boat. It cannot be possible to guard the coastline of an entire island, even if it is a small one. We know that you are a good man, DI Calder. You appreciate when to bend the rules if it is for a greater good."

Andy's eyes rolled up to the swirly, artexed ceiling, feeling that he'd been well and truly ambushed. Then he dropped his head down into his hands in a gesture of defeat. "Shit. I am going to get into so much trouble for this."

Chapter 10

When Police Scotland experienced its re-
structuring several years previously, the
Cowcaddens Road Station was effectively demoted to
a local cop shop. Each of the serious crime divisions
moved to the larger premises at Pitt Street. This was
where Dani and her team had been based for the
previous five years.

The Cowcaddens Road building looked much the
same as she remembered, a little shabbier, perhaps.
But the second floor – once the home of C.I.D – was
now used for administration. It's work stations were
populated by uniformed police constables, tapping at
glossy keyboards.

Dani wondered why she had come here. The
atmosphere wasn't at all like it had been in the mid-
2000s.

Sergeant Gray, who had been charged with giving
her a tour of the station, gestured to the floor above.
"We've not used the third floor since 2013. You're
more than welcome to go up and have a look. But be
prepared for a mess. The cleaners don't go up there
anymore either." He lifted his eyebrows. "We've had
to make cuts in the budget somewhere."

Dani smiled. She wasn't at all sure the visit
would be worthwhile. But since she was there, it
seemed remiss not to have a recce. Sergeant Gray
returned to the busy reception area on the ground
floor. Dani strode towards the lift.

As she stepped out onto the open space office
area, Dani was immediately transported back to her

days as a detective constable, first assigned to the criminal investigation department. She recalled how odd it felt to be out of uniform. To be in a skirt and blouse amongst the dark suited men who dominated the division.

Desks were arranged at regular intervals. A few were shielded by Perspex dividers but all had their own telephones. The types that had now become obsolete.

Dani realised that this floor must have been a direct mirror of the one below. She recalled now that the station had accommodated dozens of officers from around the city following the bus station bombing in 2006. The building became a hive of activity. Her own unit were central to the task of identifying the terrorists and preventing any future attacks.

Brushing her fingers through the dust that lay thickly on every surface, Dani wandered past each of the desks. She was picturing the scene as she would have experienced it a decade before: Travis, McNair, Currie, Boag. With Lowther in her own partitioned office at the far end of the floor.

Dani herself shared a desk by the window, with a view of the car-park and the constant hum of the M8 an accompaniment to every report she wrote. A grey metal filing cabinet sat in one of the corners. Dani tugged at the drawers and discovered them unlocked. There were still a few files left between the hanging dividers, presumably their contents having long ago been transferred to a computer database. She flicked through the contents, finding only one that bore Juliet's name. Dani slipped it into her bag. She would inform the desk sergeant that she'd removed it on her way out.

Turning to take in the scene one more time, Dani sighed, before stepping into the lift and pushing the button for the ground floor.

*

The property that Sean Ballater shared with his wife was in desperate need of repair. Paint was peeling off the window frames and there were ominous gaps in the tiling on the roof of the single storey building.

Gail Ballater was barely showing her pregnancy. The woman was so slenderly built that even the slightest of baby bumps was strikingly noticeable.

Calder and Mann had interrupted the couple's evening meal. Andy knew it was unavoidable, as Ballater was probably only at home to sleep and eat, and often not even for that.

As a result, Gail was bad tempered and uncooperative. "You don't need to talk to them again!" She called out from the kitchen, as her husband stood with their unwelcome visitors in the hallway. "We can demand a solicitor be present."

Sean rolled his eyes. "Come into the sitting room. Let's make this quick."

Andy perched on a well-worn sofa. "The forensic results on your boat came back clear."

Sean shrugged. "Tell me something I don't know. I've hardly got the time to be murdering women and transporting their bodies around the Small Isles."

"So, what *do* you do all day?" Alice asked abruptly. "Your wife told our fellow officers you're never here. You can't be fishing at night."

The man shifted his gaze towards her. "I have to set my pots. I've got them positioned up and down this coastline. It takes hours. I often do it by torchlight if it's late."

Gail had come to hover in the doorway. "Then he goes for a drink at the Harbour Bar. You can ask

Gus, the manager. Sean is a permanent feature in there."

Her husband cast her a disdainful look. "Hardly. But I am there on a Friday night. A working man has to let off steam somehow."

Having presumably made her point, the woman ducked out of the room again.

"I expect there are plenty of other fisherman who frequent that establishment," Andy added. "There must be a lot of talk about this murder. What's their take on how the body got there?"

Ballater seemed surprised by the change of tack. "You want my opinion, on *your* case?"

"It's more like I want to know what the local mood is. It must be difficult to work, what with the police restricting which boats can come in and out of the harbour."

Ballater's shoulders relaxed a fraction. "The fishermen talk about nothing else. The waters around Ghiant usually provide a decent catch. But the police boat won't let any of us near. It doesnae patrol after dusk, but we're no' fools. As your partner said. Nobody fishes at night."

"But you mentioned before that there are folk who sail out to the island after dark, for more recreational purposes. Are they still doing that?"

Ballater gave a wry smile. "The locals aren't stupid. We realise that you bobbies have been asking all these questions because you think that woman was killed here on Nabb and then taken to Ghiant to be dumped. But *we* know our community better than that. There are no killers amongst the fishing folk here. Just uncomplicated people desperate to make a living for their families. Which means there's a nasty murderer on the loose. So why on earth would anyone be taking a boat out to that lonely, deserted island while that's still the case?"

Andy could see the man's point. He turned towards Alice. "DI Mann, would you mind having a word with Mrs Ballater in the kitchen? Find out if she's seen anything unusual out here in the hills, or along this part of the coastline in the last few weeks. Anyone hanging around who isn't one of the locals."

When Alice was out of earshot, Andy turned back to Ballater, his voice lowered. "Listen, I know you're not involved in this murder business, so I wondered if you could assist me in a different matter?"

Ballater narrowed his eyes, a flash of interest and amusement showed in their bluey depths. "Oh aye? Run it past me, Detective Sergeant, and I'll see what I can do to help."

Chapter 11

The house in Pollockshaws was exactly as Dani had remembered it. The kitchen fittings must have been a few years old now, but they were gleaming clean and still as expensive looking.

The only thing that had changed was the layout downstairs. A large cupboard between the stairs and the kitchen had been converted into an open plan office space. This was clearly where Phil Boag was filling his days.

The ex-detective had spent the first ten minutes of her visit describing how the work had been done.

"It's perfectly positioned," Phil continued animatedly, "as I can get to the coffee machine within seconds. Speaking of which?"

Dani nodded. "I'd love one. Thanks."

Phil busied himself opening a fresh packet of beans. "I'm freelancing for a clothing firm right now. They want to expand their online business. I'm designing their sales software. To be honest, I'm inundated with offers of work."

Dani examined her old friend carefully. His face appeared smoother and plumper than when she'd last seen him, his clothing casual but well-tailored. Phil looked more relaxed. She might even go as far as to say, happy.

"How about you?" He perched on the stool beside her at the island. "I'm very sorry about what happened to Sam. With everything that went on back then, I never got the opportunity to say so properly."

"It certainly puts things in perspective."

"Exactly. I may have been leaving the force under

a cloud. But I still had my girls, and Fiona."

"I should have been round to visit you sooner. But you know what it's like. One big case after another."

Phil jumped up to pour the coffees. "I wasn't sure if we were still friends," he said quietly.

"After everything we've been through, I'd like to think so."

Phil sat back down. He looked relieved. "Good. I'm not sure that Calder was ever my friend to begin with."

Dani chuckled. "The irony is that you're probably one of the best friends he's ever had."

Phil laughed too. "Bring him with you next time. I've not been insulted in a while. I'm getting withdrawal symptoms."

Dani sipped her coffee, determined that her next visit would definitely be a social one.

Phil seemed to read her mind. "But there's another reason why you're here today?"

Dani placed the cup carefully on the sparkling granite. "Once a cop, always a cop, eh?"

"Something like that."

"Do you remember Juliet Lowther? She was a DI at Cowcaddens when we were stationed there?"

"Of course. We worked together for several years."

"She's dead. Her murdered remains were found on the Isle of Ghiant, near Skye, at the weekend. You may have seen something on the news. We've not released her identity yet. She worked for a long time on counter-terrorism cases. Much of her latter record on the force is covered by the Official Secrets Act. I don't think the DCC wanted her death becoming public knowledge."

Phil stopped drinking and dragged a hand through his thick, grey hair. "Christ. I saw the reports but didn't pay much attention."

"We've got enough murders here in Glasgow, you mean?"

"Yeah, exactly." Phil took a moment to allow the information to sink in. "Juliet left the force early, didn't she? What had become of her since?"

"She was living in a flat in Fort William, supplementing her pension by offering her services as a fitness instructor. Juliet had no contact with her family and few friends. The SIO on the murder case is struggling to find any suspects from her life."

"Can it have been a random assault? A mugging or attempted rape gone wrong?"

"Juliet was subjected to multiple stab wounds to the torso, in a location quite separate from the dump site. The perp took the trouble of transporting her body by sea to a remote and deserted island for disposal. It doesn't sound very random to me. Her ID was left on the body. Either the killer had no expectation we'd find her, or he was intending to send out a message of some kind."

"Shit. I know Juliet could be a ball-breaker to work for, but she didn't deserve that."

Dani shifted round in her seat. "What do you remember about her, Phil? You'd been in that team before I arrived. Did Juliet have enemies?"

"She played it by the book. There was the occasional run-in with DC Currie, who was a lazy bastard. I liked her, because she was efficient. My girls were very small back then and Jane was working long hours. I felt lucky to have a superior officer who had some sympathy with my situation."

"I felt that about her too. I was fortunate to have a woman above me in my first detective job. She taught me how to navigate the pitfalls. I recall her fondly."

Phil nodded. "Maybe she got herself into trouble more recently? I never understood why she went so early. The police force seemed like it was everything to her. Was she in debt? There may have been loan sharks after her?"

Dani shook her head. "Her bank accounts were healthy. No evidence of a recent jilted lover." She paused and took a sip from her cup. "I did find something amongst her effects."

"Oh, yes?"

"Well, a couple of things. The first was a certificate of baptism."

Phil got up to pour more coffee. "We've got those for the girls, we keep them with their birth certificates. It's no big deal, surely?"

"No," Dani replied carefully. "But this certificate was for an adult baptism. Juliet was baptised last year by a priest in Fort William."

Phil glanced at Dani with interest. "Was Juliet religious when we knew her?"

Dani let out a chuckle. "From the number of blasphemous phrases that escaped her lips on a regular basis I wouldn't have said so."

"She must have found religion after she left the force then. It could even have been a social thing – joining a local church to meet people."

Dani shook her head. "Juliet didn't seem to be very sociable in recent years. I don't think it can be that." She sipped the fresh coffee. "It made me think of couples who get their newborn babies baptised when they have something wrong with them. So that the child has been blessed by a priest in case they die."

"You suspect that Juliet knew she was going to die?"

Dani shrugged. "It's just a thought."

"You said there were a couple of things?"

"Yes. Amongst her insurance papers was a policy for a car. I asked the landlord of the block of flats she lived in. He claims Juliet never had a car there. I also dropped in on the lady in the flat below, who watched Juliet come and go out of her window. She was surprised at the mention of a car. According to her, Juliet went everywhere on foot or by bus."

"So, there's a vehicle somewhere. That's a lead for Highlands and Islands to pursue."

"Absolutely. I've passed on the info. The team were a little sheepish it wasn't picked up on earlier. They've got a bulletin circulating now with the licence plate of the vehicle. It's a green Ford Focus, ten years old. I reckon if we find that car, we find the murder site."

"You could even launch a public appeal. See if anyone saw the car or Juliet in the days leading up to her death."

"Yes, it might be time to break the media silence."

As if to illustrate the point, Phil was quiet himself for a few moments before suddenly declaring. "It could have been to do with the bomb."

Dani looked at him with interest. "The Roydon Road bombing?"

"Juliet's religious conversion, I mean. The incident affected all the officers involved very profoundly."

Dani shuffled forward. "What happened on that day, Phil? I was on leave with my dad on Colonsay. I only came over for the aftermath. I found a couple of files relating to it when I visited the old station yesterday. But the information they provided was decidedly thin."

Phil sighed heavily. "The girls were still in primary school. I was already mostly on deskwork, needing to be able to leave for school pick-up. I was lucky. When the reports of the explosion reached us, Juliet quickly gathered together her team: DC Currie, DS Travis and DS McNair. They were to liaise with the anti-terrorism squad when they reached the scene. But at that early stage, they were the first to arrive. The bus station was minutes away."

"It must have been chaos."

Phil nodded. "Medics were coming on foot from the hospital. Lowther and Travis had the job of clearing the area and making sure there were no further devices inside. Currie and McNair ended up performing first aid on casualties until the ambulances got there. It could only have been a matter of minutes before back-up arrived, but it must have felt like forever."

"I read there *was* a second device?"

"It was Travis who spotted it. A black leather hold-all left by one of the ticket offices. The bag was stuffed full of TNT and nails. By that point, everyone was evacuated except for the casualties on the ground and a few walking wounded. Travis radioed the bomb squad and informed them. They were still ten minutes away."

"They should've got the hell out of there and waited for back-up."

"DI Lowther decided not to cause additional panic. The poor folk on the floor couldn't get themselves clear of the second package. She and Travis decided to get as many people out as possible. They carried some between them and others they led out on foot. Remember, they thought that second bomb could go off at any moment."

Dani nodded solemnly. "Lowther received a bravery award for it. They got another fifteen people clear of the ticket offices before the techies arrived to defuse the device."

"Travis got an award too. It turned out the second bomb had faulty wiring. It was designed to detonate twenty minutes after the first, presumably in the hope of targeting the rescue workers who would have swarmed the place after the initial blast."

Dani shook her head and tutted. "Evil bastards."

"An extremist group linked to fundamentalists in Afghanistan took responsibility. We arrested the two men who planted the bombs. They'd been caught on CCTV. They were both Glaswegian, born and bred."

"I remember. I was there for the investigation. It felt like those indoctrinated boys were just the tip of the iceberg."

"They've been in prison for eleven years now. They'll never come out."

"And the victims will never forget." Dani finished her coffee.

Phil folded his arms across his chest. "I never saw what the others did. I was back at Cowcaddens Road, co-ordinating the operation and watching the events unfold on BBC Scotland. But Kerr Travis unburdened himself to me one evening in the pub. He had a young family too. There were several child casualties at the scene. Travis was in pieces, barely keeping things together."

"Did the officers receive counselling?"

"Yes, they did. I sensed that the pain eased with time, didn't you?"

Dani nodded. "Aye, I did. But I still felt our team was never the same. Juliet led our investigations in a new way after 2006. She was tougher, less compassionate."

"I was relieved when you eventually got your promotion to DI. I never hesitated after you asked me to follow you to Pitt Street when a position came up."

Dani laid her hand on his arm. "It felt like we had to get away. Juliet had taught me everything, I owed her so much. But in those last few years, it was like she was losing control."

Phil's eyes misted with sadness. "That's exactly

what it was like."

Chapter 12

The party had set out just after dusk. It was the time of year in the Highlands when it never really got truly dark. That's what Andy hoped, anyway.

Ballater had towed his boat to a landing stage nestled amongst a natural cove of jagged rock on the northern tip of Nabb. Andy hadn't known it existed. None of the locals they interviewed had mentioned it to the police. The structure was rickety and in disrepair, but still managed to do the job.

Bill kept glancing nervously at his wife. They were both wrapped up in padded jackets and had woollen hats pulled down low over their ears to keep out the chill. A bulky bag was stuffed down between the older man's feet; as if they were prepared for a natural disaster of some kind. Joy was staring resolutely ahead, in the direction of the dark silhouette of Ghiant, a narrow sliver on the horizon.

The boat surged as the tiny outboard motor powered through the gentle waves. It was a calm evening. Andy was using binoculars to scan the water, checking that the police launch wasn't still patrolling the area.

The journey took just over half an hour. Andy was beginning to realise that bringing Juliet Lowther's body here under the cover of dusk wouldn't have been too difficult a job, particularly for someone who knew the area.

Ballater jumped out of the stern and hauled the boat up the beach. Andy noticed the bulge of his muscles as he made the task look easy. The fisherman then lifted Joy clear of the boat and planted her gently on the shingle. Bill and Andy scrambled out after them.

Ballater informed his passengers that he would be sheltering in the old post office, having a cigarette. That's where they could find him when they were done.

Andy lifted the flashlights out of his backpack and handed them to his companions as they strode up the shore to the road. "Only use them in an emergency. Someone on Nabb might see the lights and raise the alarm. This is a murder scene, remember? The local police have the place under surveillance."

Bill nodded. "Of course. The moon is full tonight. We should be able to see perfectly well."

"Do you want me to come with you?"

Bill shook his head. "Can Joy and I have some time alone here?"

"Okay, fine. But don't wander too far from the road. And for Pete's sake don't get into any trouble."

"Don't worry, Sergeant Calder, we'll be perfectly okay. You really needn't concern yourself about us."

Andy rolled his eyes, feeling he'd heard that one before from the Hutchisons and learnt to recognise its foreshadowing of disaster. But he was glad of the opportunity to have a recce of the place himself. He'd not had chance to see the spot where Lowther's body was found. He usually would have by now in a murder investigation.

The detective approached what he knew to be Rushbrooke Farm from the scene of crime photographs. He could tell the stone farmhouse had once been substantial. There was evidence of several outhouses positioned up the hillside. The largest of these he knew to be the place where Lowther's body was dumped.

Andy looked back towards the beach. It was maybe a quarter of a mile away. The slope was relatively gentle. Andy tried to scan the undergrowth, looking for signs of drag marks. He cursed the lack of light. It was impossible to make out a damn thing. He wasn't going to risk switching on the torch. But he knew the teams that first examined the scene didn't identify any. Which suggested the perp was strong enough to lift the body somehow. Or there was more than one person involved in the disposal.

They hadn't lifted any shoe-prints either. The weather leading up to the discovery of the body had been windy but fair. The lack of rain meant the ground was hard. There wasn't much, evidence-wise, going in their favour.

Andy briskly walked the area around the barn. There was a copse of trees at the brow of the hill, which gently rose behind the farm. He found it odd to be in a place without any street lights. He imagined that the inhabitants left the island before they became ubiquitous. Their absence meant that the sky seemed magnified above him, the stars as clear as he'd ever seen them.

Glancing at his watch, Andy began making his way back to the road. When he reached the remains of the old post office, he saw a snake of smoke escaping through one of the window apertures, where the glass was long gone. Ballater was still there waiting for them.

Andy looked up and down the street. The moonlight was illuminating it like a landing strip. There was no sign of Bill and Joy anywhere.

Ballater stepped out of the doorway. "We need to get going soon. The wee boat will struggle if the tide is against us."

Andy felt his frustration bubbling up. He reached into his pocket and pulled out his phone, finding

Bill's number and calling it. The ring tone clicked straight onto answerphone. His friend didn't even have his mobile switched on.

Reluctant to do so, although he wasn't sure why, they were a long way from civilisation, Andy called out to the couple, striding up and down the main street as he did so, each cry becoming increasingly urgent. "Shit," he muttered under his breath as there was no response of any kind.

Ballater strode up to join him. "If we don't head back now, we'll all be here when the police boat arrives in the morning. I'm guessing you'll be in deep shit with your boss and I'll be arrested for contaminating a crime scene or some such bollocks. I'll probably find myself back up there as murder suspect number one."

Andy glanced about him in desperation. The abandoned village was eerily still. There was no sign of human life. "For Christ's sake, Bill!" He cried out one more time. "Where the bloody hell are you both!?"

Chapter 13

DI Peyton was looking more relaxed as he addressed the team. The dark blotches which had encircled his eyes for the previous few days had receded. The man had clearly enjoyed a decent night's sleep.

Which was more than could be said for Calder. He'd got back to the hotel before midnight and retired straight to his room, where he sat at the bay window and trained his binoculars on the Isle of Ghiant until the early hours of the morning, searching for signs of life.

"Thanks to DCI Bevan's detective work on the mainland, we now have a new lead. The team at Fort William have put out an ANPR check on the car that we now know was registered in Juliet Lowther's name."

"A green Ford Focus," Alice Mann clarified. "Do we believe this is the vehicle that brought our victim to the west coast?"

"I'm hoping the camera records will show us whether that is the case. What threw us off the scent initially was the fact that Lowther clearly kept the car at a location separate from her residence. Nobody knew she drove it, including her brother."

"Why would she keep its existence a secret?" Andy asked, trying to focus on the situation in hand. "The car was legally taxed and insured. It wasn't as if there was anyone in her life who would have much cared about her driving it."

Peyton furrowed his brow. "We must surmise that

Lowther was up to something she wanted to conceal. Trips to meet people that she didn't want becoming public knowledge."

"It was this secret existence that no doubt got her killed," Alice added sagely.

Peyton addressed Andy directly. "Tell me what happened between you and Sean Ballater."

The DS nearly jumped out of his seat. "I'm sorry, sir? What do you mean?"

Alice shot him an odd glance.

"What did he have to say for himself when you and Alice went back to re-interview?" Peyton clarified.

"Oh, right. I think we both concluded that although Ballater is an untrustworthy type, willing to set pots in places he's not supposed to, there's no evidence of a body having been on his premises or in his boat."

"I concur with that, sir," Alice added. "The general consensus amongst the fishing folk on Nabb is that this crime was committed by an outsider. I interviewed Ballater's wife, she's in the cottage most of the time by herself. She's noticed a few more tourists wandering up the beach near their place in recent months, but no one whose behaviour stands out."

Peyton sighed. "Then we need to strike Ballater off our suspect list." He turned to DC Tom Carrick. "Is it worth talking to the old lady again – remind me, what was her name?"

"Mrs Hutchison," Tom replied.

"That's right. We might be able to get more out of her about the island. To be honest, until the ANPR reports come in, we're treading water here."

Before Carrick could answer, Andy cut in. "I believe they've already gone, sir. I saw the husband on the pier yesterday. They were going to complete their walking tour of the Cuillins. I said it was okay. We wouldn't need them for anything else."

The young DC nodded. "That sounds about right. Mr Hutchison was obsessed with those hills. I don't really think his wife had much more to say. I thought she was a bit batty. I'm not sure her testimony would get us anywhere, boss."

Peyton sighed. "Okay, fair enough. It was worth a try. In the meantime, we search Gordon for any signs of this green Focus. DI Mann and DS Calder, can you sign out one of the squad cars and take a drive round the island, see if this vehicle is parked up anywhere? Check out a few barns and garages if you have to." He caught each officer's eye. "It would be mightily embarrassing to find out Lowther's car has been on Nabb this whole time."

Andy got to his feet. "Certainly, sir. We'll do that immediately."

*

Alice glanced across at her colleague, as he gripped the steering wheel and stared straight ahead at the narrow road which circumnavigated the island. "You look like shit."

Andy managed to crack a smile. "You don't look much better yourself."

"Do you remember that expensive single malt we drank in the hotel bar the other night?"

"Aye, it was a lovely drop."

"Well, I spent the following couple of hours throwing it up in the toilet of my en-suite."

Andy turned to look at her properly. Alice was thinner than ever, which he wouldn't have thought possible. "Maybe you should go back to Glasgow, get the division medic to take a look at you. This case isn't really our problem."

Alice smiled at his concern. "I already know what's wrong with me. It didn't require Dr Findlay and his casebook to work it out."

Andy nodded his head in dawning comprehension. "You're pregnant."

"Yup."

"Not great timing?"

"You could say that." Alice chuckled without humour. "Fergus and I have only been an item for six months."

"What are you going to do?" Andy knew this was a topic where he needed to tread carefully. He wasn't about to spill her secrets. He had enough of his own.

She shrugged. "Tell Fergus first. He was an unwanted baby. The thought that his mother could've got rid of him rather than having him adopted is something that gives him sleepless nights."

"From what I know of Fergus, I reckon he'll want this baby. The timing may not be great for you, but I sense he's ready to settle down."

Alice distracted herself by scanning the roadsides and verges for signs of the car. "I think you're probably right," she finally replied. "I might have to put the brakes on my career for a while."

"Fergus is a lawyer, he's got money. You can get childcare and come back. That wasn't an option for me and Carol. Her job didn't pay enough to make it worthwhile."

"Yeah, but Carol wanted to be at home with Amy, didn't she? I can tell she's a brilliant Mum."

Andy flushed with pride. "Aye, that's certainly true. But Amy's at school now. I'm always telling Carol she needs something else in her life."

Alice never thought she'd ever be having this kind of heart-to-heart with Andy Calder of all people. "Anyway, what got into you this morning in the briefing. You nearly fell off your chair when Peyton asked us about Ballater?"

Andy shifted in his seat, avoiding her gaze. "I didn't get much sleep last night, that's all. I sat in the bar until late."

"You'd better lay off that single malt, then. It clearly doesn't agree with you."

Andy raised his eyebrows playfully. "Well, I think that goes double for you now, DI Mann. It's strictly orange juices for the next nine months."

Despite herself, Alice laughed. She'd been foolhardy enough to confide in Calder about her condition. She was going to have to accept some serious ribbing as a consequence.

Chapter 14

The ANPR checks had generated several matches. DI Peyton relayed the results to Dani first, as she'd been the one to find the lead.

Peyton called her at her Scotstounhill flat. "There's a camera on the A82 between Glencoe and Oban. Lowther's car was picked up a few times on that stretch in the past couple of years."

Dani pictured the route in her mind's eye. "If Juliet was driving south on a regular basis, then that's the road she'd use, isn't it?"

"You think she was heading back to Glasgow?"

"Juliet had lived in the city for a long time. She must have had associates there, friends even. It's the only other place in Scotland that we know she had links to."

Peyton sighed. "If she'd taken the central route, through Glencoe itself, there are no cameras until Callender. It would be possible to weave through the back roads and not get picked up by ANPR."

"She may have taken that route more times than the checks suggest?" Dani thought about this. "What about her movements in the weeks leading up to her death?"

Peyton was smiling on the other end of the line. He couldn't help himself. "We've got a registration match showing the car entering Mallaig on the A830, at 1.03pm, just four days before her body was found."

Dani stood up straighter at this news. "Do we know if Juliet was driving?"

Peyton felt a rush of excitement as he relayed the information. "We pulled the CCTV from the petrol stations on that route between Fort William and Mallaig. We got a clear shot of Lowther filling up the Focus at the Corpach Esso station. From what we could make out, she was alone at this point."

"Juliet got herself to the west coast. This is a real breakthrough. Have you checked the hotels and guesthouses in Mallaig? Did she get on a ferry there?"

"We're working on those avenues now, Ma'am. I also have some local officers checking the town for the car. It may have been her last port of call."

"Yes, possibly. Well done, Grant, this is excellent work."

"Thank you, Ma'am. But it was you who gave us the lead."

Dani ignored the show of gratitude. She knew the real graft lay in following it up. "I'm still interviewing Juliet's old police colleagues here in Glasgow. I've got nothing solid so far, but I feel like it's important. Do you want me back on Nabb?"

"No, Ma'am, I'd prefer it if you continued to dig into Lowther's past. Andy and Alice are doing me proud here. I'm grateful to still have them to be honest."

"You've got them for as long as you want." Dani breathed in deeply. "We need to be seen to have put in our best efforts on this, Grant. I'm beginning to feel that Juliet's death is part of something big."

Peyton gulped. His excitement turning to nausea. "Okay, well, I'll keep you updated Ma'am. And thanks again."

The line was already dead.

*

Dani paced into the kitchen, reaching for the pot of coffee stewing on the worktop. James was seated at the table by the patio doors, poring over a thick wedge of papers.

He glanced up. "That sounded promising?"

"Yes, Peyton has finally got a sighting for Juliet in the days leading up to her death. His officers can now perform the enquiries we should've got done days ago."

"Does this mean you'll be going back to the island?" James tried to sound relaxed about the prospect.

Dani moved beside him and rested her hand on his shoulder. "I'm of better use here, tapping up Juliet's ex-colleagues and keeping the department running smoothly."

James couldn't hide his relief. "Good. I like you being at home. Although I know I shouldn't say that."

Dani leant down and brushed her lips across his. "Why the hell not? It's rather nice to be wanted." She sighed, "I expect Carol feels the same, though. I don't know when I'll be able to return Andy to her."

"And Alice has Fergus now, don't forget. Your team are becoming increasingly domesticated."

Dani smiled. "Alice isn't the domesticated type."

James shrugged. "You never quite know. People change."

Dani became thoughtful. "I wonder if Juliet can have changed as much as she appeared to. The DI Lowther I knew was a workaholic who abused her body with alcohol and nicotine. She liked expensive cars and gourmet meals. The Juliet Lowther we found dead on Ghiant was a fitness freak; a born-again Christian who lived the kind of frugal life a nun would be proud of."

James shifted around in his seat. "You and Phil

were convinced it was the bus bombing that changed your old DI. But she was still living that same lifestyle in Glasgow for several years afterwards. Perhaps it was something else that changed things for her. Perhaps she was forced to alter her lifestyle because of a physical illness. That can give folk a wake-up call."

Dani dropped into the seat beside him. She knew her boyfriend was speaking from experience. His mum's cancer diagnosis and treatment had shaken the whole Irving clan. "Juliet's *PM* and medical records indicated no serious health complaints. If she hadn't been savagely stabbed to death, Juliet would have lived on for decades."

"Then maybe it was the ill-health of somebody else she knew that caused the shift in lifestyle. When you see a person you love suffer, it can affect you deeply."

Dani furrowed her brow. "Juliet's mother died not long after she'd left the force. Perhaps it had something to do with that. I don't think there was anyone else in her life that Juliet ever really cared for."

"Then take a closer look at her mother's death. It might provide you with some more background info, at least."

Dani hugged her coffee cup. "Yeah, I'll do that. Because whatever caused Juliet's change of heart, I'm convinced it holds the key to why she was killed."

Chapter 15

Andy glanced around the hallway of the Celtic Thistle Bed and Breakfast. The décor was as twee as the name of the establishment. The thick carpet was patterned with a purple tartan from no identifiable clan. Amateur framed watercolours of stags in various poses lined the walls.

A lady with a chintzy apron tied around her middle stepped out of a side room. She had a guest book lying open in her hands.

"Mrs and Mrs Hutchison checked out two days ago, Detective Sergeant. They informed me over breakfast that morning. Their next destination was Rum. Bill was planning to do the Cuillin Ridge walk whilst Joy explored Kinloch Castle."

Andy nodded. At least the couple's story didn't vary too wildly from his own. "And they left with all their luggage?"

"Of course," the landlady answered indignantly. "I would have contacted them immediately if they'd left anything behind. I took their mobile phone number, just in case."

Andy knew that was useless. It'd been switched off since their voyage to Ghiant. "Did you see them when they departed the premises?"

She crinkled her brow. "Well, they settled the bill after breakfast, but I don't believe they actually left for another couple of hours." She turned her head in the direction of the rooms that lay at the rear of the ground floor. "Alec!" She boomed. "Can you come here a minute?!"

A small man with a wide stomach and thinning hair shuffled along the corridor, a newspaper clutched in his hands. "What's the to-do?"

"This is a detective, Alec. He wants to know if we saw the Hutchisons before they left on Wednesday."

He narrowed his eyes. "Marie was cleaning the rooms. I saw the couple out. Is there a problem?"

Andy shook his head affably. "Not at all, sir. We just need to verify the Hutchisons' whereabouts. They aren't in any trouble, but the couple were present on the island when the body was discovered. They were interviewed as witnesses. We really need to keep tabs on their movements."

The man raised his eyebrows. "Well, if you believe that harmless pair had anything to do with a murder, I don't have much faith in your investigation."

"No, they aren't suspects. This is purely routine."

He scratched his blotchy scalp. "They were damned fit for their age, I'll say that much. They both headed out in full walking gear. Bill had the type of backpack on that you'd only need if you were going to be living out in the wilderness for a fortnight." He chuckled heartily. "Ah, well, I suppose it pays to be prepared. We're always complaining about tourists who climb the hills without the correct equipment. It could hardly be said about them."

Andy felt his suspicions were being verified. Bill and Joy had planned their disappearing act. He was just a pawn in their game, whatever the hell that was. "Thank you for your assistance. I think we can assume that wherever they are, the Hutchisons will certainly be able to look after themselves."

The landlady frowned. "Oh, I'm not so sure, Sergeant. Bill was hearty enough, but his wife was a wee waif of a thing. I hope he wasn't being overly ambitious for them both with his plans."

Andy sighed deeply. "I really hope so too."

*

The temporary incident room was full of activity. Andy slipped back into the town hall, confident that his absence hadn't been conspicuous. He sidled up to Alice, who was peering intently at the screen of her laptop.

"Highlands and Islands have located the car."

Andy dropped into the seat beside her. "Fantastic. Where was it?"

"In a long stay car park in Mallaig. It's one that folk use if they're boarding a ferry on foot. It's cheaper than the parking facilities at the terminal. It's privately owned and at this time of the year, they never send inspectors out to check it."

"Lowther's car sat there unnoticed for over a week?"

"It seems so. The techs have taken the vehicle to Fort William. They'll be all over it, looking for forensic traces."

"Any CCTV in the car park?"

Alice shook her head. "Nope. It's just a piece of wasteland that some local businessman makes a nice few bob out of come the summer months. He never bothered putting in cameras. Punters definitely park there at their own risk."

"Maybe Lowther knew the place was lax on security. It's a smart location to choose if you want to avoid detection."

Alice twisted round. "Do you think she met somebody there?"

"I'd bet money on it."

"Her killer?"

Andy shrugged. "Any record of her taking a ferry out of Mallaig?"

Alice shifted her screen so her colleague could get a clear view. "I'm checking the manifests now. Unless she used a false name, it doesn't look like it."

"If she did get on a ferry, using a fake ID, Lowther would be sailing to Armadale, right?"

"And once on Skye, she could reach any of the Small Isles – Rum, Eigg, Canna or Nabb."

"But what if she never got on the ferry boat? The other possibility is that she met someone in that car-park and left with them in an alternative vehicle."

Alice tossed her pen on the desk in frustration. "If she did switch cars, we've no way of finding out where they headed next."

"We might still find witnesses. We're only talking about a few days ago. Mallaig is a small place."

Alice tried to look positive. "Aye, you're right. And the forensics on the car might provide us with a suspect at last."

Andy made encouraging noises. But privately he was feeling less optimistic. Juliet Lowther knew about forensic evidence and CCTV cameras. She was an ex-cop, and a high-ranking one at that. She'd kept a vehicle at a secret location for years. Lowther avoided routes with ANPR cameras whenever possible. She minimised the risks of her trips. If the woman was meeting people she didn't want anyone to know about, there was no way that Lowther would have let them anywhere near the inside of her motor.

Chapter 16

The rain had come on heavily as Dani entered the lobby of the Clyde View Rest Home in Dumbarton. A wall of heat hit her as she approached the reception desk, along with the smell of cleaning fluid and roast dinners.

She held up her warrant card. The young woman behind the desk nodded and picked up the phone on her desk. Within minutes, a middle-aged man in a suit emerged from a back office and approached the DCI with a wide smile.

"DCI Bevan, my name is Mike Dunnett, I'm the manager here. Would you like to speak in my office?"

Dani followed him into a spacious room with windows overlooking a landscaped garden.

"Now, it was Mrs Lowther that you were interested in?"

"That's right. Her daughter was a police officer and her death is currently under investigation. I understand that Juliet Lowther visited her mother here regularly?"

Dunnett nodded. "Neris Lowther joined us in the summer of 2009. Physically, she was very active, but her dementia was in its early stages. Juliet felt it was safer for her to be here rather than at home alone."

"Could you describe Mrs Lowther's condition for me, please?"

Dunnett made a steeple out of his hands. "I've got her medical notes here. Neris was quite lucid for a couple of years. She made solid friendships with other residents and took part in a variety of our activities. It was in 2012 that her condition began to deteriorate. I'd say that by the end of that year, Neris would have been unable to recognise any of the staff. I recall Juliet became quite alarmed when her mother no longer knew who she was."

"How did Mrs Lowther die?"

"As I said, Neris remained physically fit, but she suddenly began to lose weight. We brought in the doctor, who diagnosed stage three bowel cancer. Her passing was very swift. Mrs Lowther died in the December of 2013."

"How did Juliet deal with her mother's illness?"

"If you knew the Detective Inspector at all, then you'll appreciate she was a strong-willed person who didn't give much away. The cancer diagnosis was treated with matter-of-factness and little sentimentality. I sensed that Juliet found the dementia more difficult to contend with."

"Did any other family members come to visit Mrs Lowther?"

"The son came maybe twice or three times during the four years Neris was with us. I believe he lived in the United States. Juliet was her only other visitor."

Dani relaxed into the padded seat. "I'm surprised that Juliet didn't bring her mother home to live with her once she'd left the police force."

Dunnett pursed his lips, as if considering the scenario carefully. "Alzheimer's is an extremely difficult illness to cope with. I hope that Juliet realised her mother was better off here with trained professionals. I'm sure that DI Lowther was an excellent police officer, but I sensed she didn't quite have the *patience* required to nurse her mother full-time."

"You have a very nice establishment here. What are your fees like?"

Dunnett appeared unfazed by the question. "I will

print you off a copy of Neris's bill for her final year with us." He brushed imaginary dust from his lapels. "You are correct in your insinuation, DCI Bevan, our fees are higher than the state-run institutions. But the environment and care we provide here is top notch."

Dani glanced about her. She didn't doubt this was true. "I would like to see those bills now, thank you."

"I'll get Klara to make you a coffee whilst I print out the paperwork. You can take it in the drawing room. It has a lovely view of the garden. I believe the rain may even be starting to clear."

*

The drive from the care home to the anonymous estate of new build houses on the outskirts of Paisley took less than half an hour.

Dani climbed out of the car and approached a detached property with a small, newish car parked on the driveway.

A woman in her late forties answered the door. As she took in Dani's appearance, her expression seemed to stiffen, as if in resolution or perhaps acceptance.

Dani showed her warrant card, but felt that this woman didn't need it to tell her the person on her front step was a police officer.

Lorraine Travis stepped back into the hallway and allowed Dani to enter.

"I'm sorry to bother you at home, Mrs Travis. It's nothing serious, I promise."

The woman's shoulders relaxed a fraction, as she led the way to a pleasant kitchen-diner. "You must have known what I was thinking," she said simply.

"How long has Kerr been working undercover?"

Lorraine flicked the switch on the kettle before taking the seat opposite Dani at the dining table. "He's been with Vice for three years. But his current operation has lasted six months so far. If I see him once a fortnight I'm lucky."

"You thought I was coming to tell you something had happened to him?"

She nodded. "That's just how I live." Her eyes slowly took in Dani's appearance. "Have we met before?"

"I worked with Kerr at Cowcaddens Road for a few years. Then I got my Inspector badge and moved to Pitt Street."

She furrowed her brow. "I think I remember you. Your hair was very short then?"

"That's right. It was necessary for my years on the beat. I'm mostly pushing paper these days."

Lorraine got up to make the drinks. "And now you're a DCI. That's pretty impressive."

"How are your kids?"

Lorraine smiled. "One is at college and the other is an apprentice at a local building firm. Not really kids any longer."

Dani accepted her coffee and put the cup to her lips. "I was hoping to speak with Kerr. His department told me it was impossible."

Lorraine rolled her eyes. "He's *deep* undercover." She chuckled. "Sometimes I think they're just making it all up. Them and the villains, simply playing an elaborate game of dress-ups."

"I'm not sure if it isn't just exactly that." Dani folded her arms across her chest. "Do you remember a DI at Cowcaddens Road called Juliet Lowther? She was Kerr's superior officer for a few years."

Lorraine blinked several times before replying. She appeared to be gripping her cup tightly, her knuckles drained of colour. "I've not heard that name mentioned in a while. Yes, I do remember her. She came here a few times back then for drinks. Kerr liked her."

"I'm afraid Juliet was killed. Her body was discovered a week ago. She was murdered."

Lorraine's grip on her cup significantly weakened, causing it to spill its contents onto the table-top.

Dani jumped up and took the cup from her, noticing Lorraine's hands were shaking badly. "I'm sorry, I didn't mean to surprise you with this. The information hasn't been released to the public yet."

"It's just that I'm always expecting to hear that news about Kerr. The words shook me up."

Dani pulled some kitchen towels off a roll and wiped the spillage up. "I've been digging into Juliet's past on the force, hoping it might throw up a motive for her killing. I recalled that after the Roydon Road Bus Station bombing, Juliet and Kerr seemed to have developed an understanding."

Lorraine let out a grunt. "You *could* call it that."

Dani sat back down beside her. "What do you mean?"

"I thought they were sleeping together. After the terrorist attack happened, when Kerr and Juliet went back in to save people, my husband changed."

"It must have been incredibly traumatic."

"I tried to get him to talk about it, but he wouldn't. Kerr started staying out late most nights. I asked my mum to come around and stay with the kids once. Got in the car and drove to that bar you lot were always drinking in."

"Dobbie's."

"That's right. I looked in the window. I saw Kerr next to her at the bar. He was leaning into her ear, all smiles and laughs. At home, he would barely even look at me, give me or the kids the time of day. His hand was resting on her back. I knew he was shagging her."

"I never suspected anything. But then I didn't often go for those drinks. I was a bit of an outsider in that department." Dani sighed. "Did you confront Kerr about it?"

Lorraine shook her head. Tears were pooling in her eyes. "I don't think it lasted long. After a few months things got better. Kerr was home more and he started touching me again. I reckoned it was over between them. I didn't know who'd ended it and I didn't care."

"That day of the bombing, it messed everyone up. I was lucky not to have been there. Kerr and Juliet saw the worst of it."

"Is that supposed to excuse them screwing behind my back?"

"No, it doesn't. But you can't be absolutely sure they were."

Lorraine looked at Dani with an almost pitying expression. "Are you married? Kids?"

"No."

"Then you don't understand. I may not have had proof but I *knew* it was going on." She jammed a fist into her breastbone.

Dani said nothing. She still wasn't convinced. Kerr was most probably screwing someone, but she couldn't envision it being Juliet.

Lorraine seemed to have a sudden fit of conscience. She reached forward and took Dani's hand. "I'm sorry I said that about you not having a family. I've got no idea what your circumstances are, its none of my business. It's just a difficult time for me with Kerr away so much and the kids gone. It's almost worse than it was back then, after the bombing."

"Did Kerr choose to do undercover work?"

Lorraine took a deep breath. "Yes, he told me he

was good at it. He sometimes jokes that if he didn't become a policeman, he could've been an actor."

Dani pictured Kerr Travis with his dark good looks and deep, resonant voice. She could definitely imagine him on the stage. The reviews would refer to him as a 'heart-throb'. "I'm sorry to ask you this, Lorraine, but did your husband ever say anything about Juliet being in trouble? We can't find a motive for her murder, you see."

Lorraine dabbed her eyes with a ball of tissues. "I'm the last person you should ask. Kerr told me nothing about his work." She snorted. "I've probably provided you with a motive for myself. Although, I wouldn't have bothered with the woman now – all these years later." A thought seemed to abruptly occur to her. "What if she slept with someone else's husband more recently?"

Dani raised her eyebrows. They hadn't identified any evidence to suggest this.

"Because I hated her back then. After I saw them together in that bar I used to imagine them in bed together – her underneath my husband, writhing and groaning." She had started shredding the tissues in her hand, the tears now dried up. "My hatred for Juliet Lowther was so strong that I would quite happily have seen her rot in hell."

Chapter 17

Bill Hutchison rested a hand on his lower back and examined the pattern of clouds in the sky. The rain had held off for a day now, but he could tell that a heavy shower was imminent.

He bent back down over the task. The old-fashioned implement in his hands performing the job of cutting smooth rectangles of peat from the soil amazingly well. Bill didn't have long, so he slid the last deposit onto the wooden board, where the other dark brown oblongs lay, side-by side, ready to drag into the barn to be dried off. The peat would take days to dry out properly, but they might just get a smoky fire lit from it by nightfall.

Joy came out of the dilapidated farmhouse to join him. "You've done a marvellous job, dear. All that peat should keep the fire going for at least a week."

"I just need to get them into the barn before the rain comes. They'll be reasonably dry then by sundown. The lack of rain recently has left the earth parched of moisture. Which is fortunate for us."

The Hutchisons had set up camp in the living room of the Rushbrooke farm. The fireplace in there was functioning well, now that Bill had climbed onto the roof and removed a gulls' nest from the chimney. He carefully carried it down. Placing the crown of twisted twigs and feathers, filled with a lining of tiny speckled eggs, into the branches of an apple tree. Hoping the mother would discover it there.

The sofa and chairs, now damp and threadbare with age, were still in the room. Joy had placed their sleeping bags on the furniture's cushions, to provide some support and comfort. They hadn't brought many provisions with them, only enough for a handful of days – a week at the most. The water supply had long since been cut off, but Bill had brought a device that converted salt water into drinking water, which he'd purchased online. Neither of them ate much these days, so they had sufficient resources for the short-term.

What Bill hadn't counted on was the terrible cold at night. The chill winds whipped through the crumbling stonework after dark. It became essential to light a fire. They hadn't wanted to have the smoke potentially give away their position, but after one bitter night in that place they knew it was unavoidable.

It was evident that Detective Sergeant Calder hadn't reported them missing to his superior officer. Not yet.

Bill knew that the longer they were on the island, the more Calder would worry about their welfare. He would blow the whistle eventually.

Joy was walking around the edge of the trench that her husband had created with his cutting. "I can recall my uncle doing this job. His collie dog would follow after him, getting his paws covered in the mud."

"The peat is very sticky," Bill replied. "Almost like clay."

Joy glanced across at Bill. "Thank you for bringing me here. I feel so close to my family now. It's like a burden has been lifted."

Bill nodded. He thought his wife did seem brighter the last few days, despite the discomfort of their sleeping arrangements. There was something about the peace and quiet of the island that had a very healing quality to it.

As Joy was still wandering up the hillside, Bill decided to cut one more slice of the peat. Then they would have enough fuel to keep the fire going all night. The thought of this luxury sent a warm sensation through his tired limbs. Bill forced the tool into the side of the trench, resting his boot on the metal plate and using all his weight to dislodge the dense soil from the bank.

The peat slid away with ease and Bill nearly lost his footing in its wake. He steadied himself and gazed down at the side of the trench, which had slumped into the hole, as if there was nothing solid underneath to keep it stable.

A tingling sensation of dread crept up Bill's spine. He clambered back onto the bank and began to dig into the ground where the soil had collapsed. He had no spade, so made do with the peat cutter. It didn't take long for Bill's suspicions to be proved correct. The peat in this section had already been disturbed. Far more recently than when Joy's family had farmed there in the early sixties.

Beneath the shallow surface of grass and moss was a hollowed-out section of ground. Bill continued to clear the soil with his hands. The rain was falling now in fat droplets, making the soil oily and slick. He stopped when he felt material brush his fingertips, and then bone. He glanced up to look at Joy, who had reached the brow of the hill and was gazing out to sea, a contented expression on her face.

Bill sighed deeply. He knew now why they had been drawn to come back to this place. And it wasn't for the reason he and Joy had thought.

*

Something had made Andy wake-up. He got out of

bed and pulled back the curtains. The sky was still a purplish colour, as dawn had not yet broken. His vision was drawn to the outline of Ghiant on the horizon. He thought about the Hutchisons spending another cold night out there. Not for the first time, he felt a stab of guilt. He should really have raised the alarm about the couple's disappearing act before now.

Then he noticed something. At first, the dark shadow had seemed like a sliver of low-lying cloud. Andy reached for the binoculars he now kept permanently on the windowsill of his hotel bedroom.

The cloud was most definitely smoke. It appeared to be billowing from some kind of bonfire, which must have been lit on the beach near the jetty.

Andy furrowed his brow in thought. He could well imagine Bill and Joy being forced to light a fire to stay warm, but he was sure that his old friend wouldn't place the fire in a position where it was so obvious to anyone from Nabb who happened to be watching.

Then realisation dawned. He brought the binoculars up to his face once more and scanned the shoreline of the island. He couldn't make out much, but the red glow was still burning bright against the black profile of the dark isle.

The Hutchisons had lit that fire alright, he was certain of it. But it wasn't for warmth. The old bugger was sending him a signal.

Chapter 18

Andy had remained on Ghiant with the Hutchisons whilst the police launch returned to Nabb for reinforcements.

They would need a full forensic team along with the on-call pathologist from Fort William. It would take several hours for the boat to return. In the meantime, Andy had set up a cordon and had been given the task of preserving the scene.

"Why the hell didn't you just call me?" He said in frustration, pouring more tea from his thermos flask before pushing the plastic beaker towards Joy.

"I removed the battery before we left Nabb. I thought that if the phone was on, our position might be traced." Bill gratefully sipped from his own cup.

Andy rolled his eyes. "I think you overestimated what the police response to your disappearance might be. The two of you are adults, you can go wherever you like."

Bill shuffled forward on the Rushbrookes' old creaky sofa. "I hope our actions haven't got you into trouble, Sergeant Calder. We thought long and hard about our subterfuge. The decision to deceive you was not taken lightly."

Andy shrugged. "I told DI Peyton that I'd seen a fire on the beach. He volunteered the police patrol boat immediately. I didn't tell him about my role in getting you here and I hope you won't either. You're going to have to come up with your own explanation. You owe me that much at least."

"The discovery of the body seemed to occupy all

of the Inspector's attention," Bill said gravely. "But when he returns, I know there will be questions to answer." The older man tapped his nose. "Don't worry, we have a story ready. We won't grass you up."

Andy had to stop himself from snorting out a laugh. "It's the discovery you've made here that matters now. Are you sure you didn't know what was buried at your uncle's farm before you came?"

Joy shook her head. "Not at all. We were simply gathering fuel for the fire. But obviously the island was revealing its secrets to us. That's why it called on me so clearly to come back."

Andy tried to ignore the supernatural undercurrent of her words, he knew what the Hutchisons were like. "I suppose that if someone had used Ghiant as a dump site for Juliet Lowther's body, it makes sense it had been done before."

"By the same person?" Bill asked.

"I don't know." Andy dragged a hand through his hair. "Lowther's body wasn't buried like this one."

"The body in the peat is remarkably well preserved. Have you heard of the Tollund Man?"

Andy shook his head, bracing himself for one of Bill's lectures.

"The conditions in the peat bog have the effect of almost mummifying the corpse. Tollund Man died in Iron Age Denmark, yet his skin and internal organs were preserved by the highly acidic, low temperature and oxygen environment. Unfortunately, although the skin can be well preserved, often the bones are not, due to the acidity of the soil."

Andy put up a hand to stem the flow of information. "But the body you found was hardly pre-historic. The man was wearing an Adidas jacket."

"But the shorter-term implications are the same.

If the body had been in the ground for several months under normal conditions, it would just be a collection of bones right now. But did you see the face, DS Calder? It looked like the man was sleeping."

Andy edged forward in his seat, his interest getting the better of him. "So what else does the peat do to the body after death?"

"Well, the pathologist will be able to give you a better idea than I can, but from what I've read, the combination of acidity, cold and lack of oxygen has the effect of both preserving and severely tanning the skin."

"This might make it difficult to determine the race of our body?"

"Yes, I suppose so. Also, the lack of bones will make it tricky to pinpoint a cause of death. In the case of Tollund Man, his body was discovered with the rope used to strangle him still around his neck. I don't suppose that in this instance, you will be quite so lucky. I also imagine that the extraction of DNA will prove problematic."

"Great, that's all we need."

Bill leant forward. "But you will have the face. There will be someone out there who recognises him."

Andy sighed. "Only if he had friends or family in the UK. If our John Doe is an illegal or an asylum seeker from another continent, we haven't got a hope."

"But if that is the case," Joy interjected. "What on earth would he be doing here on Ghiant?"

"That's an extremely good question," Andy replied, a grim expression on his face.

*

Dani was helped off the boat by one of the forensic technicians. She crunched up the beach behind DI Peyton, who was walking with the on-call pathologist.

The rain had started again, which was the last thing they needed. A couple of SOCOs ran off ahead to set up the tent over the body, trying to minimise the potential damage the water could cause. The cadaver was only loosely covered in a tarpaulin sheet. The initial team had no idea that they were going to discover a scene of crime when they'd travelled out to the island in the early hours of the morning.

Dani left Peyton and his team to do their job, heading in the direction of the farmhouse, where she knew Calder and the Hutchisons had been holed up all day.

"Andy?" She called out, stepping carefully through a dark entrance way which was strewn with the debris of several decades of structural decay. There were even a few branches lining what was once a stone-tiled floor.

"We're in the kitchen!" He hollered back.

Dani picked her way to the room at the side of the house which contained a large oak table and a selection of Formica cupboards and appliances lying under a layer of dirt.

Bill and Joy were seated on wooden chairs at the table. Andy was watching the activity outside through a pane of glass that was almost opaque with filth and riven through with a jagged crack. He turned as Dani approached.

"Afternoon, Boss. I'm glad you're finally here. I was starting to worry I'd be stuck in this God-forsaken place over night."

"I drove straight up from Glasgow. The team were just about ready to set sail when I got to Nabb.

Peyton had to wait for the pathologist and the techies from Fort William to arrive."

"Sure. They don't have the facilities for this kind of thing on Nabb. But don't worry, nobody's gone near the body since Bill dug it up yesterday."

Dani took in the state of the couple. They were hugging plastic cups of what must have been lukewarm tea as if their lives depended on it. Joy looked exhausted. But she had to admit, her cheeks had more colour than when they'd last met.

"What on earth were you two doing here in the first place?"

Bill took a deep breath, as if preparing for a big speech. "We paid a local fisherman to bring us here. Joy needed to return to the island one more time. I'm afraid we will not divulge the name of the skipper. I worked very hard to persuade him, so I will not betray his identity."

Andy laughed hard. "You can save that speech for Peyton." He turned to address his boss. "I brought them over, Ma'am. I paid Ballater to transport us in his boat at dusk. He's got nothing to do with the Lowther murder, we thoroughly checked him out. Bill told me they only wanted to look around. But as soon as we arrived on the island, they both gave me the slip."

Dani slid onto one of the chairs. "For Christ's sake, Bill. We're in the middle of a murder enquiry. The killer could still be on this island somewhere, or return at any time. Now we've got a second body, we could be talking about a serial offender."

"Yes, but if Bill and Joy hadn't found that body, we would never have known it was here," Andy added.

Dani shot him a warning glance. "We may eventually have re-examined the area."

Andy grunted, to indicate he found this prospect

remote.

Bill's expression was penitent. "I'm sorry, Danielle. We've caused you and DS Calder all this trouble. But the call of the island was so strong. I really thought that Joy might fade away without the chance to come back here."

Joy nodded in agreement. "My dreams were becoming increasingly vivid and urgent. There was no question I had to return."

Dani rolled her eyes up to the ceiling and slowly counted to ten. "Okay. You're here now and no real harm is done. But when Peyton interviews you, stick to story one. I don't want you to mention Calder's involvement, it will only complicate the investigation."

Bill's face lit up. "Oh yes, we intend to."

"But he's going to find the situation extremely odd, so please don't start going on about the island calling you home. He'll probably bring in the division psychiatrist to assess you both." Dani was beginning to wonder if that might actually be a worthwhile exercise.

"Anything you say, Danielle."

Andy moved across the room to join them. "Bill's got some quite good knowledge about bodies buried in peat, Ma'am. It's worth hearing it."

Dani sighed heavily. "Go on then."

Bill described the case of the Tollund Man, and other similar discoveries across Europe.

Dani leant forward. "Do we think the man was deliberately buried in the peat, in order to preserve the body?"

"The preliminary examination showed no identification amongst the clothing. It's not like the Lowther case, where her ID was left clearly on show," Andy explained.

Bill looked thoughtful. "The body wasn't buried

very deeply, but then it would be very difficult to make a deeper trench in that kind of soil. The fact the body was buried at all suggests the killer did not want this man's whereabouts to be discovered."

"Unless the man died of natural causes and he was buried out of respect," Joy suggested.

"This has got to be a suspicious death," Andy said flatly. "Otherwise, you'd just call the authorities and let them deal with it."

"I don't believe that the person who buried the body understood the effect this type of soil would have on the nature of decomposition. Peaty deposits surround the farm. It would have been impossible to avoid it." Bill gazed at each of them in turn, resolution in his expression. "For your forensic department, I'm convinced this is a bonus."

Dani nodded. "You may be right. We've got a photographer out on the hillside now getting the best shots we can of the face. If we distribute the images out amongst the press, it should jog someone's memory."

It was Andy's turn to look grave. "We've found two victims already. Do we think there might be more out there?"

Dani involuntarily glanced out of the grubby window at the landscape, made grey by the continuous drizzle. She shuddered. "I don't know, Andy. We're going to have to perform a thorough survey of the area to find out."

Chapter 19

DI Peyton gazed at the photographs laid out on his desk. The death mask of the man found in the shallow grave on Ghiant reminded him of the mummy of Tutankhamun which he'd seen in a TV documentary with his wife a few months previously.

The addition of the modern sports jacket made the taut, stained skin and perfectly preserved expression of the face seem grotesque.

Dani Bevan picked up one of the shots to examine it more closely. "I think this photo gives the best representation of the features. I suggest we use it for the press release."

Peyton sighed. "As soon as word gets out that there's been another body found on the island, we're going to get all sorts of media speculation about serial killers and the like."

"It can't be helped." Dani put the glossy print back into its Perspex sleeve. "The techies are struggling to lift any DNA. We're only managing to date the victim by the jacket he was wearing. Apparently, Adidas released that limited-edition jacket in early 2008. It was on sale for six months in most sports stores across the UK. So, we know that he must have been buried after that time. But if our victim picked the jacket up in a charity shop, he could have been buried there as early as last week."

Peyton rubbed at the stubble on his chin. "Yes, but the grasses had grown over the top of the soil. It must take several months for that process of mummification to take place, surely?"

"The tech lab is co-ordinating with a forensic pathologist to get a better idea about that. Without solid bone mass, the *PM* couldn't determine a cause of death, but the pathologist felt that the skin displayed patches of damage, which he was convinced must have been caused by severe bruising."

"Where was the bruising most pronounced?"

"Around the wrists and ankles, as well as across the stomach."

"As if he had been bound and then hit repeatedly in the midriff. Whilst sitting at a chair, maybe?"

"Exactly, the kind of scenario we'd expect with a gangland interrogation or punishment."

Peyton narrowed his eyes. "I know I'm just a Highland bumpkin, but don't those types of crime tend to occur more commonly in the cities – not out here on the Small Isles?"

Dani nodded. "Quite right. If we found these wounds on a body in a warehouse in Glasgow, it would all make perfect sense."

Peyton sighed. "We're looking for a man who would have gone missing sometime after 2008? That doesn't narrow things down much."

"He was roughly 5'10" tall, the pathologist believes he was likely to be under 35 years old and of slim build."

"The jacket makes me imagine someone young," Peyton commented, "as does the face, but I'm not sure why."

"I'd say only a person in their late teens to early twenties would wear a jacket like that, but it's pure speculation. The jacket was widely available across the UK, but the main stockists were in the major cities – London, Manchester, Birmingham and Glasgow."

"He could have lived in Glasgow then, like Juliet

Lowther had?"

Dani could tell Peyton was desperate to identify a connection of some kind, to move the investigation forward. "Yes, and his remains being found here in Scotland make that more likely, but again, we have no solid evidence to support it."

"Then we need to get that photograph out in the press as soon as. With any luck, there's a family out there somewhere who will recognise their lost son, or brother, or cousin."

Dani fingered the edge of the pack of pictures once more. "I certainly hope so."

*

The lounge bar of the Gordon Hotel was as busy as Andy had ever seen it. A group of thick-set men in cable-knit sweaters were crowded around the bar area. The tables were filled with smartly dressed individuals, drinking coffee, and whom Andy immediately recognised as plain-clothed detectives. Alice was seated at one of the tables with them, deep in conversation.

The table he headed for was the one where Joy and Bill were sharing a pot of tea and scones, an incongruous sight amongst all the police activity.

"Sergeant Calder, please come and join us. I'll send for an extra cup." Bill pulled out a chair.

Andy sat down. "I hope you both got a decent night's sleep?"

"Oh, aye. The hotel is very comfortable."

But Joy looked unsure. "I've been worrying about the island, Sergeant. Will the place be overrun with diggers – churning up the earth to search for," she lowered her voice dramatically, "*dead bodies*?"

Andy smiled. "The technology is a bit more sophisticated these days." He dipped his head towards the group at the bar. "Those chaps are forensic geologists from the University of Edinburgh. For starters, they will examine satellite images of Ghiant to identify any variations in the surface which might indicate a burial site."

"The ground on Ghiant must be full of dips and troughs, won't this be an impossible task?" Bill shuffled forward in his seat.

"Apparently, these features look different from a natural change in the topography. Those guys are trained to spot the difference." One of the waiters handed Andy a cup which he filled from the pot. "Once they've located potential burial places, they can take the sniffer dogs over to examine the sites."

"Is that a fail-safe way of finding remains?" Bill looked sceptical.

"Most graves of the criminal variety are fairly shallow. The dogs have a ninety-nine percent success rate in trials. If we really want to be sure, DI Peyton could bring in ground penetrating radar. But that's going to cost us big."

"And if they find anything, that's when the digging will start?" Joy clutched her teacup tightly.

Andy nodded. "Yup, but there's no reason to imagine there will be more bodies. This is a precautionary exercise. There's no proper ferry service to Ghiant. We'd probably have to use a navy cruiser to transport the equipment over."

"Let's hope it doesn't come to that."

"The survey guys were telling me they sometimes use drones to photograph the area, that can be more accurate than the satellite images."

"It's marvellous, really," Joy seemed relieved. "I thought the island would be destroyed."

"You mustn't worry about that, Joy. Imagine the archaeological digs that take place in the most picturesque of locations. They re-fill the soil afterwards and you'd never know they'd been there."

Bill sighed. "Yes, but the police don't have such a strong reputation for making good after an investigation. Ghiant is an abandoned island. We worried that there would be no one left who would care what state it was left in. Out of sight, out of mind."

"You and Joy care," Andy put in. "The ecological brigade will care too. So, you must stop worrying yourselves about it. Wouldn't it be best if you both went home for a bit? I'll keep you updated on what's happening here. Get Louise and the boys to come and stay, keep you busy."

Joy gazed at him in surprise. "Oh, no, Sergeant Calder, we couldn't do that. Not when it's just starting to get so interesting here."

Chapter 20

Charles Lowther had requested another meeting with DI Peyton. The SIO decided that Dani should be present when he spoke with the man. The two of them had known Juliet reasonably well, he still hoped to shake out some more information about her life.

Peyton's office was too small, so they had commandeered the bay window of the Gordon Hotel, most of the officers now being busy over on Ghiant or at the team headquarters in the town hall.

Dani was surprised by how large Charles Lowther was. Juliet had been taller than average herself, and of a muscular build, but her brother's stature consisted mostly of body fat, his face slightly puffy and flushed, despite the deep tan. The resemblance was still there, though.

"I was about to book my flight home. Then I read about this other body turning up." Lowther fished a folded piece of paper out of his jacket pocket. It was the front page of the previous day's Herald. "Why didn't I hear about this straight from you, DI Peyton?"

"To be honest with you, Mr Lowther, I thought you would have returned to the U.S. by now. We are still in the process of identifying the man whose body was discovered in the peat. There is no evidence that his death is related to your sister's murder in any way."

Lowther looked incredulous. "Are you kidding me? According to this article, Juliet's body was found just *metres* from where this kid was buried. How can that be unrelated?"

Dani leant forward. "The body in the peat had clearly been there for a significant period-of-time. What happened to him may have nothing to do with the killing of Juliet. Ghiant is remote, it has a long history, we can't jump to any conclusions."

The man's tone softened. "If we were talking about downtown LA, here, I might be able to agree with you, DCI Bevan. But I've not been away from Scotland for so long that I don't realise finding *two* bodies on a wee western island is pretty damned unusual."

Peyton nodded. "Okay, we don't want to patronise you, sir. We are certainly working on the assumption that there may be some kind of connection. As yet, that link is not clear."

Charles dragged a hand through his greyish hair. "Look, I didn't intend to be an asshole about this. It's just that my wife wants me to come home straight away, but I feel like I need to stay here to follow the case – like I'd be letting Juliet down if I didn't. This discovery makes it feel like we're even further from the truth."

"Every new discovery brings us closer to finding out what happened to your sister," Dani explained. "Even if it appears baffling at first. But I see no harm in you returning home. I promise we will keep you up-to-date with developments."

Charles looked more closely at Dani. "You were the detective that worked with Juliet down in Glasgow. Did we meet back then?"

She nodded. "We did once. You had come over to visit your mother. Juliet met up with you at the department, she introduced us."

"Yeah, I remember. I expect we both looked pretty different then." He patted his stomach, as if to illustrate what had changed most about him. "You had shorter hair." He sighed. "I didn't visit my Mom enough back then, or Juliet for that matter."

"I took a trip to your mother's nursing home. I've been trying to piece together Juliet's life after she left the police force. I did wonder why she didn't take your mother to live with her when she retired. It would seem to have made more sense than traipsing down from Fort William to see her."

Charles' expression was sad. "I can hardly criticise Juliet for leaving Mom at the rest home. I was thousands of miles away. But I was surprised that Juliet didn't buy a place for them both when she moved north. It was what she always said she'd do."

"Perhaps Gail's Alzheimer's was what put Juliet off. The manager of the care home seemed to think this was the reason?"

Charles crinkled his brow, as if the idea disturbed him. "One thing you could always say about Jules, she never shirked her responsibilities. She'd dealt with far worse shit than a case of senile dementia. I can't see that being the reason."

Dani wasn't sure if it was possible to be so certain of how anyone would respond when faced with the reality of their parent's decline. But she did recognise Charles's assessment of Juliet's character. "Did your sister ever mention a boyfriend back then – another member of her team, perhaps?"

Charles nodded. "There was a guy, it was serious for a while, then it seemed to fizzle out. I told DI Peyton about it. He came out for dinner a couple of times."

Dani fished in her bag and brought out an old photo of Kerr Travis, that she'd printed off the police database. "Was this him? Tall, dark, reasonably handsome?"

Charles looked at the image closely, before shaking his head. "That isn't the guy. He wasn't as good looking as that. His hair was kinda sandy coloured. His nose was a bit crooked."

"Okay," Dani said evenly. "Thanks for the information." She sat back in her seat and allowed Peyton to run through the current status of the investigation with Lowther.

Somehow, the man's dismissal of Kerr as Juliet's lover didn't surprise Dani. She'd felt certain at the time that Mrs Travis had that detail quite wrong.

*

They stood on the harbour wall and watched as the police launch powered through the choppy waves. Three of the forensic anthropology team were on board.

Peyton leant down to catch the rope as the launch pulled up beside the quay. Andy put out his hand to help the men climb ashore. The wind had picked up and their hair was blowing about their grubby faces. Dani could tell that these men had been digging in the Ghiant soil.

"Anything to report?" Peyton asked the lead scientist eagerly.

The man put a hand up to his floppy fringe and kept it there, so he could secure the unruly mop of brown curls out of his eyes. "On the satellite image we identified an area with unusual surface patterns. It's to the north-east of the island. I can supply you with the GPS coordinates."

Peyton nodded, encouraging him to continue.

"We took some preliminary equipment over to check it out. We use a soil probe that can penetrate a couple of metres deep. We can run some basic tests at the site. It gives us a good idea of what chemical matter lies beneath." He took a breath. "There are definitely more bodies out there, DI

Peyton."

Dani felt her heart sink. She desperately hoped they weren't going to be faced with the prospect of a serial offender on the loose.

The man's expression softened, becoming almost playful. "But their fate will not be the concern of the police."

Peyton screwed up his face in puzzlement.

"We dug up a couple of the grave sites and took a look at their contents. It's actually a very significant find. The bodies are extremely well preserved for their age. We even bagged up some artefacts that had been placed amongst them."

"Their age?" Calder interrupted, becoming impatient with this young, academic type.

"Yes," the man replied. "The site clearly represents an important Viking burial ground. Those bodies are without doubt more than 1,000 years old."

Chapter 21

The trestle table, set up in the Nabb town hall, held the meagre selection of artefacts the anthropology team brought back from Ghiant.

Dani recognised what looked like crudely carved bronze knives, along with a small cup sporting some kind of decoration on the side. They were all wrapped in evidence bags and surrounded by flakes of the peaty soil which had enclosed them for more than a millennium.

DI Peyton opened his arms in an expansive gesture. "As fascinating as these objects may be, they have nothing to do with our criminal investigation. The Viking burial site has been cordoned off and experts from Edinburgh University will be invited to perform a full excavation of the area once our interest in the island had ceased."

"Are we absolutely confident there were no more recent burials on the island?" Alice enquired.

"As confident as the scientists can be. They took sniffer dogs over every inch of its surface. Apart from the two bodies we've already recovered, they found nothing contemporary. On the recommendation of the anthropology team, I've called off the search."

"What about the photograph of our dead body in the peat – any response to the press coverage?" Andy was keen to focus back on their present-day case.

"I've been on the phone to the Fort William team this morning. There's been the usual stream of phone-calls from folk claiming this man might be their long-lost relative. We've got to follow each one up to see if the dates and descriptions match. I've asked my opposite number to send over some names so we can help with the investigative work. It's a case of trawling through the databases I'm afraid, there have been dozens of calls. But it's the only way to identify our man."

"I'm happy to assist with that," Alice piped up.

"Good. Then DI Mann will liaise with HQ and assign your tasks."

*

Bill and Joy were waiting by the harbour master's office. They were both sporting padded jackets to protect them from the bitter easterly breeze which was causing the metal clips holding up the sails on the boats in the quay to jangle like chattering teeth.

Dani and Andy approached the couple from the direction of the town hall.

"Thank you for agreeing to meet us," Bill gushed, his cheeks were flushed. It wasn't clear whether this was from the cold or excitement.

"The team of scientists returned from Ghiant this afternoon," Dani began.

"Yes, we saw their boat from the hotel," Joy added.

"All they found on the island was an ancient Norse burial site. The archaeologists will be allowed in when the police have released the area." Dani reached out to lay her hand on Joy's arm. "There are no more victims over there to worry about."

Bill furrowed his brow. "Do they know from what era the burial site originates?"

"The team leader said they'd have to run some carbon-dating tests back in Edinburgh," Andy replied brusquely. "But that really isn't our problem."

"Fascinating, I wonder if this find will prove as

old as the Viking discovery in Ardnamurchan. This is most exciting. The Vikings almost certainly would have travelled between the Small Isles by boat. I suppose it is inevitable there would have been an ancient settlement on Ghiant."

"Great," Andy commented dryly. "But we haven't just stepped into an Indiana Jones film. Dani and I have got two active murder investigations to return to."

"Oh, of course," Joy replied. "But there may still be a connection between this discovery and your current cases."

"I really don't see how," Andy tried to keep his tone sounding tolerant.

Joy gestured in the direction of Ghiant, its profile presently concealed by a band of low-lying steel grey cloud. "The Isle is clearly an important, deeply spiritual environment. If the ancient civilisations were using Ghiant as a burial place for their citizens, we must assume they understood its significance too."

Bill carried on, as if echoing his wife's thoughts. "You had previously assumed that the island was chosen as a place to dispose of bodies because of its remoteness. But the discovery that it has been used as a burial ground by ancient peoples, going back thousands of years shows that there was clearly more to the choice of location than just that."

Andy's expression was incredulous.

"The island is sacred," Joy added simply.

"If the place is so magical, why dump a murder victim there?" Andy snapped.

Bill shrugged his shoulders. "I'm not sure how this fact fits into your investigation, Sergeant, but you must bear it in mind."

Dani nodded, deciding it was time to encourage the Hutchisons to return to the warmth of the

Gordon Hotel. "We will take this into account, I promise."

Bill put his arm around his wife's shoulders and grinned triumphantly.

Dani took the opportunity to hustle them in the direction of Nabb's main street. The couple strode off ahead, their brisk pace indicating a positivity of purpose.

"I'm not sure we should encourage their crazy theories, Ma'am," Andy muttered to his companion.

"I know, but so often the Hutchisons' insights have assisted us in the past. We dismiss them at our peril."

"Okay, you're the boss. But the pair might really have lost it this time. The stunt they pulled with me on the island the other night was a step too far. They could both have died of exposure out there."

Dani sighed heavily. "I agree with you. But our best approach is to humour them. If the pair are safe and sound at the hotel, dreaming about ancient burial rituals and Viking long-ships, we shouldn't have anything more to worry about."

Chapter 22

DC Tom Carrick was applying a method to the way he was sorting through the responses they had received to the photograph of their peat John Doe. The information he was trawling through was heart-breaking. Just about every poor soul in Scotland with a missing male relative had got in touch with Fort William MIT after The Herald published its piece.

Before he did anything else, Carrick scanned through the details, searching for the date these individuals disappeared. If it was before 2008, the print out got a red-line straight through it. Sadly, they didn't have the time or resources to inform these people not to get their hopes up. Their agony was set to continue.

The process had at least halved Carrick's list. It was haunting to read how long some families had been searching for a loved-one. In a few instances, it was over thirty years. But the young detective didn't have time to dwell on this. He examined his revised list carefully. He would be ringing each and every contact number to check on details such as height, build and ethnicity. Carrick sighed, taking a sip of tepid water from the plastic cup on his desk, in preparation for the lengthy task ahead.

*

The wind had died down along the northern shores of Nabb. Sean Ballater decided it was calm enough to collect in the lobster pots he'd placed along the pebble beach that could be reached from his cottage. He'd put on thigh length waders over his trousers and a woollen sweater to complete the task. He would usually take out his wee boat, but the tide was low enough to manage it on foot. The worst that would happen would be that he got a little wet.

Ballater had noticed all the activity taking place on Ghiant over the past few days. A visit to the bar by the harbour had provided him with an explanation. That crack-pot old couple had dug up a body on the Rushbrooke farm. Now the whole island was being turned over looking for more. He'd make a point of asking the Glasgow detective what they'd found. He'd be sure to tell him on the hush-hush, the guy had too much to lose if he didn't.

The waves were lapping up to his midriff by the time Ballater had reached the first of his pots. The current was stronger than he'd anticipated. He wrenched open the door of the trap and pulled out a couple of wee nippers which he shoved into a waterproof sack secured over his shoulder.

It took the fisherman a while to re-set the trap, the waves were threatening to lift him off his feet. The clouds had also moved in, making it feel as if dusk had already fallen. His stomach felt empty and he yearned for the stew his wife was preparing as he'd left the cottage.

Regretting the decision not to bring the boat, Ballater waded against the current towards the outcrop of slatey rocks where he knew his next cluster of pots were positioned.

As Ballater ran his hands along the smooth rock, searching for the feel of the rope which was securing the stash of pots within a natural recess, he felt a sudden surge in the tide. Wondering if a motorboat might be passing through the bay he looked up to the horizon. He saw nothing, bending back into his task once again.

The water was now nearly up to his chest which was tight with frustration. He just couldn't find the place where he'd set the traps. Crouching down, so that he could feel the cold water seeping through the wool of his sweater and gushing over its cable-knit neckline, gathering at the belt of his trousers, he finally rested his fingers on the rough plait of the rope.

"Thank Christ," he muttered irritably.

Before there was a chance to check his catch, Ballater felt his legs sweep away beneath him and his head go under the waves. The fisherman pumped his legs in an attempt to regain his footing, but a force gripping his shoulders was holding him down.

Just as Ballater felt the fight going out of him, the grip was released. He shot out of the water and gasped in the sea air; coughing and spluttering intermittently. Before there was a chance for him to turn on his assailant, Ballater felt the force of that grip on his shoulders once again, dunking him back into the ice-cold sea. This time he was more prepared, managing to gulp in a lung-full of air before he went under. But this only meant that whoever was holding him, clocking this, kept him down for even longer.

When Ballater was released the second time, he managed to rasp, "why are you doing this? What do you want from me?"

There was no reply, his head was simply shoved back under the water, if anything, more roughly this time.

The truth was that Ballater knew why this was happening to him. He understood only too well. He also knew exactly how it was going to end.

Chapter 23

Dani stood at the top of the shore, gazing down at the efficient way the forensic team were examining the area around the tarpaulin tent they'd set up on the beach to shield the body from the elements. The sky was the deep, dark blue of twilight, but two powerful arc lamps lit the crime scene.

She turned to Calder. "It was his wife who found him?"

Andy nodded. "Aye, Gail Ballater was preparing dinner when her husband informed her he was going to bring in the catch from his lobster pots along the shore here. When it got dark and the meal was cold, she headed down with a torch to search for him."

"The body had been washed up on the beach?"

"That's right, the tide was coming in at the time, but the currents in this bay tend to deposit debris along the rocky headland where Ballater's body was discovered."

"Do we think it was a straightforward drowning?"

Andy sighed, kicking the pebbles under his boot. "We'll have to wait for the *PM*. But the doc at the scene seemed to identify all the tell-tale signs of drowning – white froth at the mouth and nose, blueish tint to the skin. His body was washed up before much bloating had been able to take place."

Dani shook her head in disbelief. "But it's hard to imagine this was purely an accident, not with everything else that's been going on."

Alice Mann marched across the shingle towards them. "A WPC has taken Mrs Ballater back to the cottage, she's going to ring her mother, but the family are several hours drive from here."

"Poor woman," Dani muttered. "Andy tells me she's pregnant?"

"Yes, Ma'am," Alice replied levelly. "Nearly five months."

"Bloody hell. This will be tough on her."

Alice narrowed her eyes. "She said something odd, Ma'am, as I was making her a cup of tea and trying to get her warmed up."

"Oh yes?"

"She was mumbling to herself, but I could just about make out what she was saying. It sounded like, "I knew he'd do this, I knew he'd leave me like this." She sounded more angry than sad."

Andy looked up sharply. "The wife thinks he killed himself?"

Alice nodded. "I believe so. I suppose it's possible he simply walked into the sea."

Andy furrowed his brow. "Each time I interviewed him, Ballater seemed overwhelmed with the responsibility of supporting her and the bairn. He was exhausted with all the extra work he was taking on. It's not unimaginable that it all got too much."

Dani screwed up her face. "I just don't buy it. The man was too tied up in that island for this to be a coincidence." She zipped her jacket up to her neck. "I'm going down to view the body. I don't even know what this guy looked like."

When she reached the tent, DI Peyton was about to give the order for the body to be placed in the mortuary bag.

Dani lifted her hand. "May I just take a look, first?"

"Sure, there's no hurry. We won't be able to get him on a boat to the mainland until the morning."

She stepped gingerly forward, aware there was no way the shingle under her feet could be preserved as evidence. The tide would be in again in a couple of hours. Dani crouched down beside the broad shoulders of Sean Ballater and leaned in close.

His blue eyes were open. The froth bubbling around his mouth and nose were the first thing Dani noticed. But the second thing was the crookedness of that nose. Like the man had spent his youth on a rugby field, or in a boxing ring.

She twisted on her haunches. "Grant, can you come here a sec?"

Peyton strode forward. "What it is Ma'am?"

"Do you recall what Charles Lowther said about his sister's lover? That he was sandy-haired, with a crooked nose?"

Peyton bent down and eyed Ballater's lifeless features one more time. He turned towards one of the tech officers. "Get a few more close-up shots of his face would you, Mick?"

*

Gail Ballater was hunched over the kitchen table. A tartan blanket had been placed around her shoulders. She was gripping a large mug of dark brown tea.

Dani pulled out one of the chairs and sat beside her. "Mrs Ballater, I know this is a really difficult time. But I need to ask you some questions."

Gail shrugged. "Go ahead."

"How long have you and your husband lived here on Nabb?"

"Since we got married, that's nearly ten years ago now. Sean wanted to be a fisherman like his father was. We saw the cottage come up for sale. It was cheap enough for us to buy."

"Where did you both live before that?"

"I was a nurse, at the Royal Infirmary. My parents still live in Sighthill."

"The *Glasgow* Royal Infirmary?"

"Of course." Gail looked up for the first time, meeting Dani's gaze. "Why does that matter?"

"I'm not sure if it does. What about Sean? Where did he work before you came here?"

"He did odd jobs, short-term building contracts mostly. I don't think my parents ever really thought he was good enough for me."

"Sean never worked for the police?"

Gail tipped her head to one side. "Why do you ask that?"

"I just wondered if he might have had a reason to be mixing with police officers, back when you lived in Glasgow?"

Gail's expression became thoughtful. "No, he was never in the police. But he did have a desire to help others – do his public duty, you know? Although recently you would never have realised it." The woman's voice cracked, tears were now escaping onto her pallid cheeks.

"In what way did Sean perform a public duty?"

The middle-aged WPC gave Dani a stern look, as if she felt the interview should end there.

Gail took a breath, trying to curb her sobs. "When we first met, Sean was a fireman. He volunteered for the station near the polytechnic. You know, the one on Cowcaddens Road?"

Dani nodded, resting her hand on Gail's arm. She did know it. When she worked at the police station there, she passed it every single day.

Chapter 24

The Caledonian Hotel was across a busy road from Fort William railway station. Dani parked on a side street and approached the entrance.

The building was made from traditional sandstone and the lobby decorated in an old-fashioned but classy manner. The restaurant could be found beyond a long corridor, carpeted a deep burgundy and with stag-heads protruding from the walls.

Charles Lowther was seated at a table by one of the tall windows, the afternoon sun's low rays were placing his features in shadow. Dani took the seat opposite him.

"Thank you for agreeing to see me again."

Lowther shrugged his broad shoulders. "I'm just sitting in my hotel room most of the time, waiting for news about the case."

Dani decided not to beat around the bush. She brought a file out of her bag. It contained the photographs taken on the beach at Nabb Bay. She selected one which only showed Ballater's face. "Is this the man that you saw Juliet with back when she was working in Glasgow?"

Lowther slipped on a pair of designer reading glasses and examined the image closely. "It was a long time ago, Detective Chief Inspector, and this man's features have been distorted by death."

"I realise that. But the crooked nose is still evident, and the sandy hair and pale colouring."

Lowther nodded. "Yes, it could have been him.

Although I'd struggle to provide you with a definite identification."

Dani fished in her pocket for another photo, this one was a print of one of Sean and Gail's wedding shots. The man looked younger in this one, his sandy hair cropped neatly around his ruddy face. "How about this? It was taken a decade ago."

Lowther took the picture from her. "Yes, this is the man Juliet went out with. This picture must have been taken around that time."

Dani nodded. "His name is Sean Ballater, he married his wife in the summer of 2007. She had been a nurse at the Royal Infirmary and he was a volunteer fireman at the station on Cowcaddens Road. What made you believe that Juliet's lover was a fellow police officer?"

Lowther removed his glasses and set them down on the crisp white tablecloth. "If I'm honest, I may have assumed it. Her boyfriend had the same mannerisms as the colleagues of my sister's that I'd met previously. I'm sure they talked about cases together."

"Okay, well, Ballater was never a cop, but I believe that his and Juliet's paths may have crossed in a professional capacity. This may be why you assumed he was a fellow police officer."

He shook his head in puzzlement. "And now this man is dead too?"

"His *post-mortem* indicates death by drowning, it could have been an accident. But I agree with you. This can't be a coincidence. Sean Ballater provides the link between Juliet and the islands that we were looking for."

"Do you think Juliet travelled to the Small Isles to meet with Ballater? Could they still have been lovers?"

Dani sighed. "She could have been meeting him,

certainly. But his cottage and boats were examined closely after her body was discovered. The man had been eliminated from our inquiries. No evidence linked him to Juliet's death. The forensic tests on her abandoned car didn't indicate the presence of another individual either. It seems she was assiduous in making sure whoever she met with, didn't travel in her vehicle."

"Then does this discovery bring us any closer to finding out what happened to Jules?"

Dani nodded. "It provides us with new lines of inquiry. If Ballater wasn't the person who killed Juliet, perhaps it was her murderer who killed them both."

Lowther considered this for a moment, pouring water into a crystal glass and sipping it slowly. "Then the reason for their deaths may lie back in Glasgow, not here at all?"

Dani gave a sad smile, impressed that the man's line of thought was mirroring her own. "Yes. Juliet and Sean were lovers for a short period of time. Something brought them together over a decade ago. We need to find out what that was."

"Well, if there's anything I can do to assist you in finding that out, you only need to ask."

*

Andy emerged from the Harbour Bar feeling miserable. He'd interviewed most of the fishing community on Nabb over the previous few hours. Sean Ballater was clearly well liked on the island. Nobody was claiming he had an enemy in the world.

He strolled back towards the hotel. Alice was standing in the lobby, examining the evening's food menu which had been laminated and pinned to the noticeboard.

"Feeling hungry after our busy night?"

Alice glanced over her shoulder. "One minute I'm ravenous and the next I'm ready to retch my guts up. I've also got to avoid the sea-food, soft cheese and the chicken-liver paté starter."

"I'd say it's worth avoiding those anyway, especially in this establishment."

Alice chuckled. "Any results from interviewing the locals?"

"Sean was a decent bloke, according to his fellow fishermen. He was in the bar most Friday nights, good for a laugh, and helped out friends when they needed it. Most of them were saddened by his death."

"No motive there to want him dead, then." Alice sighed. "I'd say Gail was the one person on the island most hostile towards him."

"And now he's gone, she's fallen to pieces."

"Left alone with a baby on the way." Alice automatically placed a hand on her own belly.

Andy lowered his voice. "Have you spoken to Fergus yet?"

"We've chatted on the phone, but I've not told him my news. It seems more appropriate to discuss the matter face-to-face."

"Aye, I expect you're right there."

Andy felt a movement behind him.

Bill Hutchison was emerging from the dimly lit residents' lounge. The detective immediately wondered how much the man had heard of their conversation.

"Good evening, Detectives. Will Joy and I have the pleasure of seeing you at dinner?" Bill dipped his head towards the menu board that Alice was still poring over.

"Aye, Bill. We've not got the time to be frequenting the finer restaurants of Nabb."

"Oh, good. We'll see you later then." Bill paused. "Joy and I were woken by all the commotion in the night. It was difficult not to be."

"Then you'll know a man was found dead further up the coast from here." Andy was determined not to give away any other information.

Bill nodded gravely. "Young Sean Ballater. One of the waitresses told us at lunch. News travels fast in a small community such as this. What a shame, he was clearly a very *helpful* individual."

Andy rolled his eyes, hoping that Bill wasn't going to let something slip about their clandestine trip to Ghiant in front of Alice.

Bill carried on, "of course, somebody that willing to assist others might well find themselves wrapped up in situations which could turn out to be extremely dangerous. *Who pays the ferryman*? And all that. It would have been difficult for the man to remain separate from the *jobs* he did." He tapped his nose in an exaggerated way.

"Where's Joy?" Andy asked gruffly. "Shouldn't you be checking on her, Bill?"

"Oh yes," he replied. "I'll go and see if she's ready to dress for dinner."

"You do that," Andy rumbled, watching the man ascend the stairs.

"What the hell was he talking about?" Alice hissed under her breath.

Andy shook his head in annoyance, "It's nothing. You know the nonsense they both spout." But much to the detective's irritation, he recognised there was a tiny hint of truth in what Bill Hutchison had said.

He just wasn't exactly sure how to pursue this nugget of truth about Ballater's activities without dropping himself right into the shit.

Chapter 25

The traffic on Cowcaddens Road was at a standstill. Dani craned her neck to see what the hold-up was ahead. There seemed to be no reason for the jam except the sheer volume of traffic heading in the direction of the university and bus depot.

As soon as the opportunity arose, Dani swept her car onto a side street, finding a tiny space on double-yellow lines and sticking her police ID badge in the window. She continued the rest of the way on foot.

The Fire Station was in the same location as it had been ten years ago. Today, the huge twin garages, housing the two engines stationed there, were firmly closed. Dani was meeting the station manager, Oliver Jameson.

She pushed open the door to the reception area, showing her card to a middle-aged man behind the counter.

"Good Morning, DCI Bevan," he replied, leaning forward to offer her his hand. "I'm the manager. We only have a skeleton operational staff right now, so no task can be considered too lowly." He raised his arms to highlight his current occupation.

"I appreciate you agreeing to meet with me. You must be busy."

"Come upstairs to my office. We can talk in there."

Dani followed Jameson up a modern staircase to

an open-plan landing with sofas and coffee tables positioned at regular intervals across the floor. This large area was empty except for one man, reclining on a chair and watching the news on a television set bracketed onto the wall. His feet were in thick yellow socks and his legs outstretched in front of him, ankle over ankle. Jameson nodded in recognition of his presence.

"We've only got a couple of crew on duty right now. This is usually a quiet time of the day. I'll have a full house by six."

The office was smaller, the desk strewn with paperwork.

"How long have you been the manager here?" Dani sat on a swivel chair and wheeled it in closer.

"I was a member of the volunteer crew until 2010. Then I applied for a permanent management position. I've been doing this job ever since."

"The man I'm interested in was a volunteer here some time before 2007."

"Aye, so you said on the phone. I would have known him then."

"Sean Ballater. He moved away when he got married, becoming a fisherman up in the Small Isles."

Jameson nodded slowly. "I certainly knew Sean. We were good mates back in the day."

"I'm sorry to have to tell you that he died a couple of days ago. Mr Ballater was drowned off the coast of Nabb."

Jameson looked genuinely shocked. "Jeez, that's awful. He can barely have been forty years old. Poor wee Gail."

Dani sighed. "It's a tragedy. But not the only one to befall the islands in the past few weeks. A body was also found on Nabb's twin island of Ghiant. The victim was an ex-police officer. We believe that Sean

Ballater knew her from his time here in Glasgow."

Jameson narrowed his eyes cautiously. "What was her name?"

"Juliet Lowther. But when she worked at the Cowcaddens Road Police Station, she was DI Lowther."

The manager's features had turned pale. "Sean would have known her, yes. The whole team did back then, after the bombing, I mean."

Dani got a notebook out of her bag. "You'd better tell me the full story, Mr Jameson."

He rubbed his face, as if drying it with an imaginary towel. "When we got the call-out back in the May of 2006, informing us there'd been an explosion at the bus depot, all volunteers were expected to come in immediately, whether they were on duty or not. Sean and I were among a group of about fifteen men who responded to the bombing."

"It must have been very difficult," Dani added carefully.

"It was. There were fires that needed putting out from the initial explosion. Sean and I worked on that. We manned the hoses until we got the blazes under control. After that, the primary need was to get members of the public away from the building, which was probably structurally unsafe."

"Did you go into the bus station to bring the injured out?"

Jameson nodded, his brow had beaded with sweat, although the temperature in the room was cool. "We worked with the police officers from Cowcaddens Station. The area needed cordoning off before the bomb squad arrived. We received the news that another device had been identified in the ticket hall."

"DI Lowther and DS Travis continued to bring members of the public out of the ticket office, even after a potential second device had been located. Did any of your firefighters do the same?"

Jameson sighed heavily. "I didn't know any of the police officers' names back then, I learned those later, when we were given our bravery awards. I knew there were cops still bringing folk out, but our crew supervisor told us to man the cordon. He was very insistent about that. To be honest, there was a lot of chaos. Smoke and debris everywhere and people screaming – in pain and panic, running for their lives. It was hard to know who was doing what."

"And Sean Ballater, was he on the cordon with you?"

Jameson crinkled his brow. "He was definitely there for a while, but like I said. It was hard to keep track. In the end, myself and my colleagues were assisting the paramedics with first aid. We did whatever we could."

"You met DI Lowther after the terrorist attack?"

"We were all invited to a ceremony at the City Chambers six months later. There was a drinks reception after the awards were given out. Our entire watch received medals, along with the paramedic team and a few of the cops. Sean and I spoke with the woman police officer afterwards. We had a few drinks together, discussed the problem of terrorism, that kind of thing. An event like that, it creates a bond between those who witnessed it."

"I can imagine. Did Sean see DI Lowther after this event?"

Jameson shifted uncomfortably in his seat. "Will knowing this really help Sean and his wife? Can't we let him rest in peace?"

"Not really, sir. It appears likely that Sean's death wasn't accidental. If I can prove a connection with Juliet Lowther's murder, then I've got a better chance of finding his killer."

Jameson sighed, wiping his hands down his trousers. "I could see that Sean was getting on well with her. I think he went home with her that night."

"Was Sean with Gail at that time?"

"Yes. Gail was a nurse at the infirmary. They'd been going out for a few years. But before they married, Sean slept around. He often picked up women in bars."

"Did you think this liaison with DI Lowther was just a one-night stand?"

"I knew it wasn't. Sean talked about her for a while. He told me how much more experienced she was, compared to Gail. If you know what I mean?"

Dani nodded. "I know what you mean."

"It lasted maybe six months. I put it down to the shared trauma. Nobody else understood what we'd been through that day in 2006. Only those who'd suffered it too. I experienced a rocky patch with my wife. She wanted me to snap out of my bad mood. I felt like she existed on another planet."

"Why did Sean and Juliet's relationship end?"

"I genuinely don't know. For a while, I thought Sean might ditch Gail for good. Then he produced the engagement ring he'd bought for her and never mentioned Juliet again. Within a few months, they'd tied the knot and were off to live in the Highlands. I barely heard from Sean after that."

"Could you put some dates down in a statement for me? Then I can get an idea of when the relationship between Ballater and Lowther started and ended."

Jameson nodded. "Sure, not a problem."

"I'll make you an appointment at the station first thing in the morning." Dani stood up to leave.

Jameson cleared his throat. "Will Gail have to know about all this? I don't believe she had a clue about Sean's other women."

Dani wasn't certain this was true. In her experience, women in Gail's position tended to turn a blind eye. "Hopefully, not. But this is a murder inquiry. If we have to upset Mrs Ballater along the way, I'm afraid that's unavoidable."

Chapter 26

With the police officers busy at the Nabb town hall, the hotel was quiet. Bill and Joy had ordered morning tea in the lounge. Lining the walls of this room were a series of tall bookcases. Joy had already scanned the shelves and selected herself a dog-eared crime novel which she was reading at the table by the bay window.

Bill had slid a weightier tome from a bottom shelf. He'd already spent an hour a few evenings back, skimming through its pages. This morning, he planned to give its contents more attention.

Joy eyed her husband over her half-moon reading glasses. "What's so interesting in there? You've barely spoken a word in the last hour."

Bill lifted the heavy book, so she could see the front cover. "It's a history of the Small Isles during the war. There is a section on Nabb and Ghiant. I noticed it the other day when I was in here."

"I didn't think the islands played much of a role in the war at all. We're too far north of the Clyde for this area to have been a target for the Luftwaffe."

"That's true, but there was a great deal of German U-boat activity off the coast of the Outer Hebrides. According to this book, some of the submarines even ventured along The Minch. The aim was to target passenger ships heading across the Atlantic to New York and Newfoundland."

"What role did Nabb and Ghiant play in the war, then? My uncle's family still farmed on Ghiant back in those days."

Bill sipped his coffee. "Being the most westerly, Ghiant had a lookout point on one of its beaches. They scanned the sea for signs of enemy shipping. There was a small consignment of soldiers based on the island for much of the war."

Joy took off her glasses and allowed her paperback to slide onto the table. "I didn't know that. Uncle Rob was in the army, that's how he met my aunt. But he was stationed away from Ghiant. Are you telling me he could have stayed at home for the duration of the war?"

"It doesn't work like that, darling. Rob Rushbrooke would have had to go wherever he was posted. You couldn't pick and choose. Where did he serve?"

Joy furrowed her brow. "I'm not sure what division he was in. My father would have known, but I never asked. Family history says Rob met Aunty Catrin at the army base in Kinross. Catrin was in the ATS. They remained in contact for the entire war and were married once it was over."

"It would be easy enough to look up Rob's service record."

"Do you think he may have spent some time back on Ghiant, before the war was over?"

"I've no idea. I'm mentioning it purely out of interest. This discovery of the Viking burial ground on the island just got me thinking, that's all."

"You thought that Ghiant might have a more chequered history than we previously imagined?"

Bill leant forward and dropped his voice, quite unnecessarily, as there was no one in the room except them. "We told DCI Bevan that we believed Ghiant was special. That there was a spiritual significance to the place. If that's true, it will possess a unique history, these places always do."

Joy's expression crinkled with concern. "But it's

recent history hasn't been so good, has it? My memories of Ghiant are all idyllic. The magic I associate with the place is a force for good. What if we discover that the island has been used for evil? We already know some of its darker secrets."

Bill stretched his hand across the table and took hers. "This is just a bit of harmless research, darling, to pass the time whilst the investigation continues. Whatever I find out will be from a long time ago."

Joy didn't answer. She knew that Bill couldn't be stopped once he was on one of his crusades to un-earth the truth. But this time she was decidedly uneasy about the subject of his research. The Isle of Ghiant was so closely wrapped up in the history of her own family that she feared what his digging might uncover.

*

DC Tom Carrick had a revised list of names. He'd followed up on over thirty responses to their newspaper appeal to identify the body discovered in the peat on Ghiant.

DI Alice Mann approached the table where Tom was at work. "How is it going with the print-out I gave you?"

Tom showed her his notepad. "I've eliminated all these calls, Ma'am. Currently, I'm focusing on this list. The missing individuals referred to here match our deceased man in physical characteristics and in relation to the date of their disappearances."

The details scribbled in the margins impressed Alice. "Have you contacted the families of all these men?"

Tom cleared his throat. "I've spoken with a couple of dozen so far, I'm really sorry I haven't got through all of them just yet."

Alice shook her head of straight auburn hair. "Don't apologise DC Carrick, this is good work. I like your systematic approach. You need to check and double-check each name listed here, we don't want to miss anything."

Tom couldn't prevent a smile from lighting up his fresh face. "Thank you, Ma'am."

Alice straightened up. "In fact, I'm going to get a couple of the other DCs to come and work alongside you. They can provide you with their lists and you can inform them of your method to whittle it down. I'm putting you in charge, DC Carrick. Don't let me down."

Tom's chest swelled with pride, "Thank you, Ma'am, I certainly won't." Then his elation faded, as he realised that the already significant task before him had just expanded considerably.

Chapter 27

Phil Boag had pushed back the doors which divided the living room from the impressive kitchen of his Victorian terraced house in Pollockshaws. The dining table was set simply, but elegantly, with a pair of candles flickering in the centre.

It was a couple of years since Dani had seen Fiona Riddell. The woman looked well, which was unsurprising as their paths had previously crossed under difficult circumstances. Dani felt the situation was a little awkward, socialising with Phil and his partner like this. Her team had been required to treat Fiona as a suspect herself in the disappearance of her teenage daughter three years ago. If there was any residual bad-feeling, Fiona was managing not to show it.

Phil was busy at the stove, stirring a shrimp risotto, occasionally adding a splash of white wine to the pan. "Georgie is out tonight," he called over to his guests. "We've got the place to ourselves."

Dani turned to her hostess, who was topping up their glasses. "How is Maisie?" The question had to be asked, better sooner than later.

Fiona smiled. "She's in her first year at the university. Maisie was living with her father, but chose to come back to Glasgow to study. She stays with us most weekends."

Dani noted how happy Fiona sounded about this fact. "I'm glad she's doing so well."

Fiona laid a hand on Dani's arm. "You did your best to find her, I know that."

James changed the subject. "I love this house. Did you have it completely refurbished?"

Phil carried over the risotto in a serving bowl, adding a sprinkling of fresh samphire to the top of the dish. "It was Jane who had all the work done. I'm not sure we would have gone for anything quite so grand."

"How is Jane?" Dani felt she should ask, as Phil's ex-wife had been a feature of his life for over twenty years.

"Still the headmistress at Newton High School. But I think she'll move into local politics once the girls have completed their studies."

"*Really*?" James raised a glass of red to his lips.

"Oh yes," Phil replied, with amusement in his tone. "Jane has plenty of ideas about the future of education."

"She seems perfectly contented on her own," Fiona added. "There hasn't been anyone new on the scene since the divorce."

Dani nodded. Jane Boag had always been married to the job. She would have made a good copper, better than Phil in that respect. "I'm sure our paths will cross at some point. The DCC loves schmoozing with the big decision makers of Glasgow."

Phil chuckled, "that part of the job I won't miss. The politics and the cronyism."

Dani leant forward, her tongue loosened by the wine. "Is there anything you do miss about it?"

Phil relaxed into his high-backed chair and looked thoughtful. "I miss the camaraderie. There's nothing like the police force for making you feel part of a gang – except the army, maybe."

Dani nodded. "But it can be pretty isolating to feel on the outside of that gang."

"Were you ever made to feel on the outside for

being a woman?" Fiona asked.

"Yes, in the early years I really was. The current investigation we're working on has reminded me how different it was. The police officer who was murdered on Ghiant a few weeks ago was one of the only females on the force who could provide me with a role model when I started out."

"Was she a good role model?" James asked.

Dani considered this carefully. "Juliet was tough and she taught me how to run a high-profile investigation. But now we've delved further into her private life, I can see that she was a bit of a mess back then."

Phil rested his fork on the edge of his plate. "The officers at Cowcaddens were hard drinkers. There was a caucus who went to the bar every night after work. I needed to come back home for the girls. I knew this meant I was never fully accepted there."

"The same went for me," Dani added. "I was never comfortable in the smoke-filled backrooms, but Juliet seemed to thrive in that environment."

Phil frowned. "I always felt being a young woman went in your favour in that respect. The lads let you off when it came to their more brutish rituals. Besides, half of them were desperate to get you into bed. They just thought I was a pussy."

Dani's mouth fell open. "I don't think that's true, Phil."

"I heard the locker-room banter, Dani. When they weren't comparing one another's pin-ups of Linda Lusardi, they were discussing which females in the station they'd most like to have sex with."

Fiona snorted. "That I can well imagine. I don't think the world has really changed so much in the past decade. I suspect most men have similar conversations when they're on their own together."

James laughed. "Hang-on, we aren't all lecherous

Neanderthals!"

"No," Phil interjected, "but in the police force there is still a strong macho culture."

Dani sighed. "I can't deny that, but look at my team. I've got Alice, Sharon and Dan in key roles. The tide is gradually shifting."

Phil nodded. "Sure, I agree that the culture will change. It was different at Pitt Street anyway. I remember the relief I felt when I got away from CID at Cowcaddens Road. The atmosphere had become unbearable in those last couple of years. It was like we were waiting for some kind of terrible storm to break."

Dani took another swig of wine. "How did the officers talk about Juliet, when you were in the locker room together, stripped down to your boxers and sharing a can of Lynx?"

Phil grinned. "It was never quite like that." His expression became serious. "Juliet was respected. It was like she'd become sexless to them. Maybe she delivered too many bollockings over the years to be viewed as an object of desire to those lads. Although she was attractive, it was like the DI was out of bounds."

"Did she ever mention a man called Sean Ballater to you? He was a volunteer fireman who attended the scene of the bus bombing. It looks like they were lovers some time towards the end of 2006?"

"I don't think so, but then I can't imagine Juliet confiding something like that to me. We weren't close enough."

James cleared his throat. "Hey, this isn't supposed to be an interview room." He stood up. "Can I help tidy away the plates?"

"I'll give you a hand," Fiona said.

When the others were in the kitchen, chatting and filling the dishwasher, Dani turned back to her old colleague, lowering her voice as she said, "I think Juliet may have been sharing information about the terrorist investigation that followed the bus bombing."

"With this fireman guy?" Phil had also dropped his voice.

"Yes. They met at the awards ceremony for the emergency workers who attended the scene and quickly became lovers. Juliet's brother thinks they discussed police cases together. Now the two of them are dead."

Phil shook his head in puzzlement. "We signed the official secrets act before we investigated the boys who placed those devices in the bus depot, and the networks they belonged to. Nothing ever leaked out, not even to the press. Would Juliet really have shared confidential material with a guy she'd been sleeping with for five minutes?"

Dani shrugged, watching James and Fiona as they approached the dining table, carrying in the dessert on a large platter. "She was pretty out of control during that time, so I think we need to consider she very well might." More loudly, Dani declared, "wow, that cheesecake looks fabulous, did you make it yourself?"

Fiona smiled with pride. "I did. It took me most of the afternoon, mind. Phil isn't the only one who cooks around here."

Dani reached for a slice. "Then let's not allow all that hard work to go to waste!"

Chapter 28

Dani had liaised with the anti-terrorism squad on a few past cases. She was always relieved when her brush with that particular division was over. The DCI never liked the secrecy which surrounded their investigations and the way that standard procedures could be bypassed in the treatment of suspects. It made her uncomfortable. It didn't feel like what she'd signed up for when joining the police.

Chief Superintendent Ali McNair had worked in anti-terrorism since 2009. He was one of the officers responsible for implementing the Prevent strategy in Scotland. Dani had seen him interviewed on television about it.

McNair's office was on one of the top floors of the Pitt Street Headquarters. He had his own secretary, who escorted Dani to the door, slipping away quietly after the detective was safely inside.

McNair moved around his desk and put out his hand. "Danielle. What a pleasure to see you again. I've followed your career closely."

Dani smiled. "And I yours, sir. You've gained quite a high profile in the media."

He gestured for her to sit. "It's a major part of my remit these days. Now, what can I do to assist you?"

"As you will be aware, I'm involved in the investigation into Juliet Lowther's murder. My inquiries have involved examining her prior record as a detective."

McNair nodded. "Ronnie Douglas has been keeping me informed. The discovery of her body was quite a shock."

"A second body has been recovered on the neighbouring island of Nabb. The dead man was a local to the islands, but it has come to light that he knew Juliet when she was stationed at Cowcaddens Road, at the same time you and I were in her team."

McNair's expression remained fixed. "What is this man's name?"

"Sean Ballater. He was volunteering as a firefighter in the Sighthill area between 2006 and 2007. He attended the Roydon Road Bus Station bombing. We believe this is how he and Juliet met."

"I've never heard his name before."

"You attended the scene too, along with DI Lowther, DS Travis and DC Currie?"

McNair nodded. "I did. It was the worst experience of my career, but very much the reason I'm in my current position."

Dani raised her eyebrows quizzically, wanting the man to continue.

He shifted forward, clasping his hands on the desk in front of him. "The investigation that followed the bombing was my first experience of working in counter-terrorism. You will recall what it was like. We worked hard to identify the two men who planted the bombs. Then there were months of intensive searches of their internet connections and networks. I found the work fascinating and felt it made a real difference."

"How has that early investigation impacted on your current role?" Dani was genuinely interested.

"The remit of the Prevent Strategy is to identify the propagation of extremism before it reaches the point where terrorism is an outcome. I visit mosques and schools, build relationships with community leaders." He sighed heavily. "We are still under the continual threat of terrorism, but our approach must be to look to the future, rather than always watching our backs."

"I don't recall that kind of forward-thinking attitude being at the forefront of our investigation into those boys who planted the bombs at Roydon Road. DI Lowther and DS Travis particularly, seemed focused purely on retribution for the victims."

McNair looked saddened. "There were many flaws in the way we responded to the 2006 bombing. The investigation that followed should not have been run by those so close to the tragic events. Lowther and Travis acted with great bravery that day, but this involvement clouded their judgement."

"In what way do you believe Lowther's judgement was clouded?" Dani was trying to recall the details of the investigation. At the time, all she could remember doing was trawling through pages of computer and phone records, listing down examples of repeated activity, particularly in the run-up to the bombing itself. She passed these details on, someone else had looked into it further.

"The bombers who were subsequently convicted were only 17 and 18 years old. It was clear that they had been manipulated by a wider network. We did our best to pin something on those individuals who had fed these boys with the ideologies that made them commit the atrocity, but it was hard to make the evidence stick. I was often concerned the interviews were conducted to bully and frighten, rather than to exact usable information."

"Did Lowther bully suspects herself?"

McNair looked uncomfortable. "I should be careful what words I use. All I mean, is that the approach several officers took to the predominantly Muslim associates of the bombers that we interviewed after May 2006 would be deemed too heavy-handed these days. I certainly learned lessons from that period."

"I believe it's possible that Juliet Lowther shared the details of that investigation with Sean Ballater. He was her lover during the summer of 2006."

McNair furrowed his brow. "That information was strictly classified. Not even every member of the team knew the names and addresses of suspects."

"I know. I've tried to locate DS Travis, to interview him about that time. I've been told by Vice that he is deep undercover and won't be contactable for months. Is there any chance you could get me at least a phone call with him?"

"I'll do my best, Danielle, but I have no real jurisdiction over the operations of other divisions, despite my rank." He scratched his balding head. "Do you have any idea what particular information was passed on to this man, Ballater?"

Dani shook her head. "I'm afraid not. I only have the testimony of Juliet's brother, who cannot recall any details, only that he assumed Ballater was a fellow police officer as he and Juliet appeared to discuss cases."

"There was only one case that mattered during that period."

"Precisely."

"Do you believe this breach of security played a part in the murders of Lowther and Ballater?"

"I've got to assume so, sir." She cleared her throat. "In order to continue with my investigation, I'm going to need access to all the material Lowther had in relation to the bus bombing, sir."

McNair said nothing for several minutes, clearly considering this. "Counter-terrorism is an area of policing that never truly stops. Many of the interview transcripts and lines of inquiry from 2006 still remain relevant today. Groups who were of interest in Glasgow back then are still under surveillance now."

Dani gulped. "I understand that, sir."

"You were on the sidelines back in 2006. Are you prepared to be given the full picture now?"

"I don't think I have a choice, sir."

"Then if you are prepared to sign a copy of The Official Secrets Act, 1989, I will organise a secure place for you to view the classified documents."

Dani nodded solemnly. This was a development she didn't welcome, but she knew it wouldn't be possible to solve Juliet's murder without accepting it was inevitable.

Chapter 29

The double-poster bed of the honeymoon suite of The Gordon Hotel was covered with sheets of handwritten notes and reference books lying open, multi-coloured post-it notes marking the pages.

Joy felt it was fortuitous that this had been the only suite left available to them after they were rescued from Ghiant. It gave the couple plenty of space to carry out their research.

The dressing table was functioning as Bill's desk, at which he was transcribing notes from the screen of his laptop computer. Joy perched on the edge of the eiderdown, reading a history of western Scotland.

Bill shifted his eyes from the screen. "Do you want to know what I've discovered so far, darling? To be honest, it's a bit of a puzzle."

"Of course."

"Your uncle's service history was easy enough to find. The information is stored on the genealogy website I subscribe to." He lifted one of the pads of paper scattered about the desktop. "Robert Rushbrooke, born on the Isle of Ghiant in 1917. That's him, isn't it?"

"It must be. I expect he was born at home. Many island babies were in those days."

"Rob joined up in the first month of the war. He wasn't a conscript. He was a member of the Scots Royal Regiment, in their infantry division."

"Did he see action abroad?"

Bill shifted round in his seat. "You see, that's the

puzzle."

Joy frowned in rebuke. She was not in the mood for one of her husband's beloved quizzes.

"Rob Rushbrooke is listed here as a private in the II Corps of the Fourth Army. They were a force 250,000 strong based in eastern Scotland to prepare for an assault on German controlled Norway."

"But that makes sense, because Uncle Rob was certainly based at Kinross for long enough to meet my aunt."

Bill got up and moved across to sit beside his wife on the bed. "I know a little about the *so-called* 'Fourth Army'. I've read about it in the past. But just in case I'd got it wrong, I double-checked my facts in these history books I picked out from the library downstairs."

Joy could feel her mouth had gone dry. "What do you know about it?"

"Well, the Fourth Army was part of what became known as the 'British Deception Formations'. They played a prominent role in a propaganda war against the Germans. The British Army created a number of fictional army formations and battle plans to fool the Axis High Command. There never was a plan to invade Norway via Scotland, but the rumours kept German units busy along the west coast, ready to resist such an invasion. It was all really rather cleverly done. Radio communications were broadcast giving the impression that hundreds of men were protecting key positions, in fact there were none, or just a handful of personnel sending out misinformation."

"I don't understand, how does this relate to Uncle Rob's regiment?"

Bill placed his hand on Joy's and gave it a squeeze. "It means that the Fourth Army *never existed*. Rob's service history is a fiction, created at the time by the British Army."

Joy shook her head in frustration. "Then what on earth *was* he doing during the war?"

"That's the big question, darling. What was he doing indeed and how do we find out now, after all these years have passed?"

*

The flat in Scotstounhill was in darkness. Dani vaguely recalled James telling her he was going for dinner with his sister, who was in town for the weekend.

Dani dropped her small suitcase in the hallway. She wondered if it was worth unpacking it yet, but decided it probably wasn't. She may have to return to the Highlands before McNair got her access to the classified documents she wanted.

The kitchen cupboards were bare. It wasn't surprising, as they'd both been so busy with work. Dani found a packet of crackers open on the worktop and brought the cheese out of the fridge. She was about to pour a glass of wine when the phone in the hall rang.

She padded into the semi-darkness to answer it. "DCI Bevan here."

"Dani. It's been a very long time."

She caught her breath. "Kerr Travis. I wasn't expecting McNair to get authorisation for a call so quickly."

"He's a big hitter these days. Who'd have thought it, eh?"

Dani smiled. "Yes, his career really took off."

"He'd got the bus bombing to thank for that. Counter-terrorism turned out to really be his thing."

Dani detected a hint of rebuke in his tone. She didn't have time to analyse it. "I don't know if you heard, but Juliet Lowther was killed. Her body was found on a remote island off the coast of Skye. I've been looking into her murder, interviewing her past colleagues. Because of my connection to her."

This statement was met with silence.

"Kerr? Are you still there?"

"Yes, I'm here. It's a shock, that's all. I don't have access to the news where I am."

"Listen, I expect I don't have long to talk to you. I need to know what you and Juliet were up to in those months after the bombing. I spoke to Lorraine, she thought you and Juliet were sleeping together."

The man grunted. "You know that's not true."

"Of course, but I could hardly tell your wife that."

"What, that it was *you* I was sleeping with back then, not our boss?"

Dani cleared her throat. "Exactly. Besides, maybe you had a thing with Juliet too, I don't know."

Kerr's tone became clipped. "Don't be ridiculous, you know I wasn't."

"I'm sorry, I do know that. But there was something happening with you and Lowther. I remember how thick you both were. There were elements of that operation I knew nothing about."

"You should be grateful that was the case. What we experienced in the ticket office of the bus station that day, it changed everything."

"McNair practically accused Lowther of bullying suspects in interviews. Did you witness that?"

"The times were different then."

"So, you did witness that?"

"Do you ever think about us, Dani? The way it was back then? I wanted to leave Lorraine for you."

Dani shook her head, exasperated. "No, it was years ago. I thank God I took the transfer to Pitt Street when I did. I had no wish to break up your family. I was young and awestruck and you were very attractive and attentive. That's it."

"How did Juliet die?" His voice sounded suddenly distant.

"Multiple stab wounds to the upper torso. She bled out. The murder site was separate from where the body was dumped. The job was professional."

Kerr let out a gasp. "Poor Jules."

"Kerr, did Juliet do something back then that made her a target for this? I remember how out of control she was becoming before I left. Did something happen after I was gone?"

"The bus bombing hardened her. She had little sympathy for the pathetic self-justifying perps who crossed our paths in the months that followed. But we always stuck to the rules, you know that."

Dani could feel her frustration rising. "There's got to be a reason for her murder. I don't believe it relates to her retirement, she barely put a foot wrong in Fort William, was hardly living any kind of life at all."

His voice had drifted away once more. "Listen, Dani, I've got to go. There's nothing more I can tell you. But it's been good to hear your voice."

Abruptly, the line was dead. Dani was left with the distinct feeling she'd been told nothing at all.

Chapter 30

The impressive stone townhouse lay on a crescent overlooking the Forth. DI Alice Mann parked the car in a residents' bay and placed a police badge on the dashboard.

She turned to her companion. "I'm going to ask you to lead the interview. Are you okay with that?"

DC Tom Carrick nodded. It was his investigative work that had led them here. This was the lead which fitted best with the information they had on the identity of their peat 'John Doe'.

Alice opened the car door. She gazed up at the castle which dominated the skyline. Alice had studied at Stirling University herself. She had fond memories of the place.

Tom made sure he had the file of documents secure in his grasp as they approached the front door. Within seconds of knocking, it was opened.

An Asian man in his early sixties hovered in the doorway, he seemed almost hesitant to allow them in. "DI Mann and DC Carrick?" He ventured.

"That is correct, sir." The officers held up their warrant cards. "May we come inside?"

The hallway was tidy and flamboyantly decorated with oriental vases and oil paintings in gold frames. The detectives were led into a bright, open-plan kitchen where a lady in a beautifully stitched salwar kameez, of a similar age, was filling a high-spec coffee maker.

"Mr and Mrs Mahtam, we are grateful that you agreed to meet with us."

Izad Mahtam indicated they should take a seat. "We are grateful to you. This is the first time we have had news from the police in nearly ten years."

"Would you mind explaining the circumstances of your son's disappearance for us?"

Izad sighed. "We have of course been through this umpteen times already with different officers over the years. If it helps find out what happened to Adnan, I suppose it is worth repeating."

"We have read the police reports," Alice added. "But it really is better for us to hear the details from you and your wife."

Izad nodded. "I am a professor of law at the university here. But when our son went missing, I was a lecturer at the Caledonian University in Glasgow. Our family house was in Sighthill."

Rabia Mahtam brought over the coffees and set them down on the table in silence.

"Adnan was twenty years old in 2008. He would have turned thirty next year." He reached across to a shelf and selected an ornately framed studio shot of a handsome young man with thick, wavy dark hair.

Tom took the picture and examined it closely, passing it to Alice.

"Our son was studying Business Management at the same university where I worked. He was in his second year. Adnan had been staying with some friends on the campus of GCU. One of them called us up when he didn't return back to their flat one night."

"When was this, Mr Mahtam?" Tom asked.

"The night of 12th March, 2008. Adnan lived with us most of the time, so his friends assumed he had returned to our house instead. It was good of them to check, otherwise his absence would have gone unnoticed much longer."

"Who was the last person to see your son?"

Rabia replied this time. "Adnan was in a finance lecture the morning of his disappearance. It finished at 11am. He chatted to a couple of fellow students before leaving the faculty." He eyes misted. "This was the last time he was seen."

Alice leaned forward. "What about CCTV coverage of the campus and local streets? There are dozens of cameras in that area, I know it well."

Izad pursed his lips. "We were never shown any CCTV footage. I certainly mentioned it to the officers in charge of his case. I was told it had been examined and there was no sign of Adnan."

Alice frowned. This seemed unlikely. The boy couldn't have disappeared into thin air. The last sighting they had of anyone was usually the grainy image lifted from a CCTV recording.

"What did the police investigation conclude?" Tom asked, sipping his sweet coffee politely.

Izad clasped his hands together tightly, as if trying to fight against a rising anger. "My son had friends at a mosque in Baird Street. The officers jumped on this information immediately. Added to this, we returned as a family to Lahore every couple of years. This was viewed as suspicious by the authorities. The assumption was made that Adnan had returned to Pakistan full-time, with the intention of training with the Taliban. Once this idea was in their heads, the search for my son ceased."

Tom nodded. "Was there any substance to that suspicion? Did your son display any signs of radicalisation when he lived with you?"

Izad blinked several times, obviously trying to remain calm. "Adnan was a good Muslim. But he loved being Scottish. He had plans to become a businessman after college. Adnan had friends who were angry about the NATO presence in Afghanistan, but it is possible to associate with people who possess alternative views without subscribing to them yourself."

Tom lifted the file sitting in his lap and placed it on the table between them.

They all gazed at it in silence for a moment.

"The reason we have come here, is because you responded to the photograph we printed in the Herald. The case of your son's disappearance proved the closest match we had to the body we found buried on Ghiant."

Tears were streaking down Rabia's cheeks. "It was our daughter, Zakia, who encouraged us to call the number. She is a lawyer now, younger than Adnan would have been. She has more faith in the authorities than we have."

"Do you recall what your son was wearing on the day he went missing?"

Izad answered, his wife had her head buried in her hands. "A blue sports jacket and jeans. His trainers were Nike, I believe. Sportswear was the fashion for him and his friends. This is already recorded in his case notes."

"But do you remember the brand of the jacket, sir? It's very important."

He closed his eyes, thinking about this. "It was Adidas, I'm sure. He'd bought it only a week or so before he went missing, from the big sports shop in the St Enoch Centre."

Alice glanced at her colleague and nodded her head.

Tom took a deep breath. "Mr and Mrs Mahtam, I'm very sorry to inform you that we believe we have found the body of your son." He slipped the photographs of the boy's clothing out of the file, positioning them so that the couple could view the images clearly.

Izad's controlled expression crumpled. Rabia tipped her head back towards the ceiling and wailed.

The officers gave the couple a few moments to

recover from the initial blow.

Izad reached out and placed his hand on Tom's arm, gripping the material of his jacket so that it creased. "This news is very painful to receive. My family will take it hard. But I thank you for coming here. We believed that our plight had been forgotten, our *son* had been forgotten. Now we can bury him properly. That means everything to us."

Chapter 31

The room Dani had been given was small and dimly lit. It possessed a tiny window, high up in the wall. She had her suspicions it had once been an interview room, designed to intimidate its occupant.

The officer who showed her in didn't go as far as to lock the door behind her, but Dani still felt uncomfortably like a captive. She'd been given an hour. If she required longer, there would have to be another application to Chief Superintendent McNair for a slot.

There was no time to lose. Dani opened the thick file and scanned through its contents. Now, she had a name to search for. Adnan Mahtam, a twenty-year-old student at GCU who visited a mosque near the university campus in 2006/8.

The Baird Street Mosque was mentioned several times in the investigation papers. One of the bus station bombers had been a regular visitor there. It was clear Juliet Lowther believed he had been radicalised through his connections at the mosque. A number of individuals were brought in for questioning in relation to the bombing. Adnan's name wasn't amongst them.

It was the transcripts of the interviews themselves that had caught Dani's attention. Most were conducted by Lowther herself, with Kerr Travis in attendance. The young men being questioned all had a duty solicitor present, but there was little evidence of intervention by their legal representatives.

The questions began fairly straightforwardly, with Lowther sighting phone and e-mail contact between the interviewee and the suspect, probing for evidence of collusion in the planning of the attack. But when these questions got nowhere, Lowther and Travis became more aggressive in their approach. They hinted that non-cooperation would result in the interviewee's homes being raided by the anti-terrorist squad, armed with guns and batons. One of the young men wept at the idea of this, explaining how his mother wasn't well and such a terrifying intrusion might kill her.

Dani raised her eyes from the documents. Their contents were disturbing. This was the official account of how information was gathered during that investigation. She wondered what the hell went on informally, when they visited homes and mosques, or battered down doors in the middle of the night, without a solicitor present or a tape-recorder preserving their actions for posterity.

She glanced at her watch. There wasn't much time left. Dani jotted down the names of all those interviewed. Adnan wasn't mentioned in these papers at all. By the time of his disappearance, in March 2008, the Baird Street Mosque interviews had stopped. Lowther and Kerr were working on other lines of inquiry, gathering the physical evidence needed to secure their two suspects' conviction at the trial, which took place at the start of 2009.

Dani tried to remember her role in these investigations. She was never invited to sit in on interviews or to view the forensic evidence that the bomb squad had retrieved from the scene. Her job lay in analysing the phone and computer data, a task which didn't allow her to join up any of the dots. What she knew about the case against those accused of planting the bombs at Roydon Road in

2006 was what Juliet Lowther told her.

But she'd also had another source of information during those months. Dani had begun a relationship with Kerr Travis not long after she joined Cowcaddens' Road CID. He was married with young children, but by his behaviour you would never have known it. They were in the bar most evenings after work. Kerr helped Dani get to grips with the transition from uniform to CID.

One of the reasons Dani had been on leave with her father on Colonsay in the spring of 2006 was to reflect on her relationship with Kerr. It felt like things were getting serious between them. Kerr had talked about leaving Lorraine. Dani wasn't sure she wanted that. It hadn't been her intention to break up a young family. In truth, she'd not properly considered the consequences of what she was doing with him.

When Dani returned from Colonsay, everything had changed. In the aftermath of the bombing, the focus of the department was solely on finding the culprits. She and Kerr met a few more times in hotel rooms, but they both knew it was over. Kerr had seen children the age of his own killed or horribly injured in the blast. Even for him, this was a wake-up call.

Although they'd once been lovers, she and Kerr never discussed the details of the investigation in private. It was obvious from the moment of Dani's return that Kerr and Juliet were drawn to one another after their experience. They had their heads bowed at the desk in her office and stood side-by-side at the bar in Dobbie's. It was no surprise that when Lorraine saw them together, she interpreted this bond as an affair.

Dani knew it wasn't. It was stronger than that. She'd had an affair with Kerr and knew how little it meant compared to what he and Juliet had gone through. They'd formed a mutual support group. No one else in the department had a look-in.

Dani jumped at the sound of the knock. Her escort had arrived. She closed the file carefully and got to her feet. It didn't seem necessary to examine the documents again. The significance of them was perfectly clear.

Chapter 32

"Tell me more of what you remember about him."
Bill hooked his arm through Joy's. A gentle breeze blew across the shore, sending up the white sand in tiny spirals. The outline of Ghiant was clear on the horizon.

"Uncle Rob was a physically strong man. I suppose it was his farming background which made him that way. The summer I stayed with him and Aunty Catrin, he was always out in the fields. The job was very physical."

"You recall him as a kind man? He showed affection towards you and your cousins?"

"Oh, yes. He adored Aisling and Rory. Life on the island seemed to suit them perfectly."

"Did it always suit your aunt? She was used to living on the mainland. She played an important role in the war. Didn't she feel isolated out here? They can't have had many friends."

Joy considered this. "I don't know. She was in the kitchen mostly, cooking for the family. She helped on the farm when necessary. I suppose I assumed she must be blissful, living in such a beautiful place with a handsome, dashing husband."

Bill cleared his throat. "Was that perhaps your adolescent self, projecting her own feelings onto your aunt?"

Joy blinked several times, as if trying to make an image come clearer. "You may be right. They were terribly upset when they had to leave Ghiant for good, that much I know for certain. But Catrin lived a long, happy life on the mainland while Uncle Rob was dead within the decade."

Bill took a deep breath. "It was an old army colleague who got Rob a job on the mainland in the early 60s, wasn't it?"

Joy nodded. "Yes, the island was becoming increasingly difficult to farm for a profit. This opportunity gave Rob and Catrin a reason to leave and start again."

"Presumably, this man served with Rob in the war. He may be able to shed some light on Rob's service history. You don't happen to recall his name, do you?"

Joy glanced across at her husband. "Oh yes, I see what you mean. Actually darling, I do."

*

DI Peyton waited for the team to assemble in front of the stage in the Nabb town hall. Alice and Tom had arrived back from Stirling that afternoon.

"The identification of our peat man as Adnan Mahtam is a significant leap forward." He nodded towards Tom Carrick.

The young DC tentatively climbed the steps onto the stage. "The Mahtam family have positively identified the clothes the body was found in. The dates of the student's disappearance match the forensic evidence we have. The techies inform us that he was buried a few hours after death and had been in the peat for several years, judging by the degree of mummification that had occurred. Adnan Mahtam was last seen in a lecture theatre at GCU. He was a long way from home, winding up here. The family are professional and articulate. They put pressure on the local force to step up their investigation. Their son's participation in a nearby mosque did not go in his favour. The officers in charge assumed he'd returned to his parents' homeland of Pakistan, to attend a Taliban training camp."

Andy put up his hand. "So, this lad was living in Glasgow when he went missing. He had links to the Baird Street Mosque which was tied up in Juliet Lowther's anti-terrorist investigation. Does this mean we are now treating the two murders as connected?"

Tom glanced at his boss, "yes, I'm assuming so. The information was passed on to DCI Bevan and the team in Fort William as soon as we had confirmation of identity from the next of kin."

Alice stepped forward. "Juliet Lowther's body was dumped on the island a few weeks ago, Adnan Mahtam's body had been in the ground for several years, according to the forensic tests. He could even have been buried there not long after he went missing in 2008. We're talking about a gap of nearly ten years. That's going to be difficult to account for."

"But it can't be a coincidence," Peyton added. "These two bodies have a strong circumstantial connection, although DCI Bevan can't find any evidence yet that Lowther ever came into contact with Mahtam during the course of her investigations."

"What about Sean Ballater? Do we think he may have known Mahtam?" Andy asked.

"Can you speak to his wife again, Andy? See if the name rings a bell."

Andy nodded. "Sure, I'll pay her a visit this afternoon."

"Alice and Tom, I need you to re-examine the Glasgow Division's investigation into Mahtam's disappearance in 2008. Find out who led it and what kind of effort they put into locating the lad. We must discover how that poor boy ended up here on Ghiant, hundreds of miles from home, tied to a chair and beaten to death."

Alice was already on her way to one of the desks. "We'll get on it right now, sir."

Chapter 33

The small ferry navigated the sheltered bay of Loch nan Ceall, arriving at the village of Arisaig at midday. Bill and Joy had travelled as foot passengers. This route from Nabb was a popular one with tourists. The boat lingered for a while, so the passengers could watch for the sleek, arched back of a whale, venturing near the surface of the loch. The couple walked down the gang plank onto a compact wooden pier, taking in the beauty of the place as they proceeded.

The cottage that Joy's aunt and uncle had moved to in May 1962 was along a narrow road nestled within woodland, a short walk from the main village. The address they were looking for turned out to comprise a single-storey stone building with a neat garden surrounding it.

"The place seems tiny compared to Rushbrooke Farm," Bill commented. "You mentioned the family received compensation from the government for their re-location?"

"That's what my mother told me. She never said how much. I don't expect it was any kind of fortune, especially judging by the simplicity of this cottage."

They lingered for a while, until they saw movement behind the lace curtain hanging in one of the windows and decided to move off, before the current resident called the police. The couple strolled along a path that took them uphill, in the direction of the station.

"Rob was offered a job at a sawmill positioned on the road north. My research indicated that it was used by the Forestry Commission, to control the woodland in this part of the highlands." Bill pointed ahead, before referring back to his map.

"The job was very labour-intensive," Joy explained. "They didn't have the machinery then that they do now for felling trees and chopping wood. But it was a steady salary. My cousins could attend the local school and made friends in the village. Aunty Catrin got a job at the bakery."

They walked for another half an hour before deciding to have lunch at one of the hotels on the waterfront. They sat at a table in the window, where they could see the yachts bobbing in the pretty bay.

"I could imagine the Rushbrookes being very happy here. Ghiant is a remote place. The conditions would have been especially harsh in winter."

Joy sipped her lemonade. "Yes, I suppose I didn't think about that when I was a young girl. The romanticism of the place clouded my judgement. This would have been a very pleasant area to raise a family."

Bill brought his laptop out of the rucksack, placing it on the table and powering it up. "As you informed me, Rob's army friend was called Murdo Dunn. He was the manager of the sawmill from 1960 until his retirement in '75. I'm sure it was to his advantage to encourage a hard-working, skilled farmer such as your uncle to come and work for him."

"Did you manage to find out anything about Murdo's war record?"

"I made a start. I had to verify his birth date first." Bill tapped some instructions into a search engine and summoned up the site he wanted. "I'll add his details to the genealogy site I subscribe to, it's got a very detailed database."

Joy nodded patiently. She was used to her husband's family research.

Bill frowned. "I can't find his details listed here."

"They may not hold every record, darling. We might have to go to the archive in Edinburgh to find out more about the man."

Bill grunted in frustration. "I can usually discover just about everything I need these days from the internet."

"Try a general search. Perhaps he's been mentioned in a book or an article."

Bill looked up from the screen and glanced at his wife, impressed with her good thinking. "Yes, I'll try that. Then I will make an appointment online at the archive. It looks like we may be heading home sooner rather than later."

Joy gazed out of the window, she wasn't sure how to feel about this. Not when there were so many questions left unanswered about the island.

The sandwiches arrived and they ate in silence. Bill was absorbed in the searches he was performing on the computer. Joy didn't chastise him for continuing to work while they ate. She was just as keen to know what he might discover.

Finally, Bill pulled the laptop shut. He sat back and folded his arms across his chest, an odd look on his face.

"Come on then, what have you found?"

"Murdo Dunn was mentioned in an article, several of them, in fact. There was a flurry of pieces written in the press in the late seventies and early eighties, when the documents from World War Two were first declassified. He's mentioned in a few of those."

"Declassified?"

Bill nodded. "It seems that Murdo Dunn was an officer in the secret services during the war. He was in SOE to be precise. I expect his own family never knew the details of his experiences in those years."

Joy shook her head in confusion. "But Dunn was an army colleague of Uncle Rob. How would their paths have crossed?"

"Well, I can only conclude that Rob was a spy as well. That would explain why the war office gave him a fictitious service record."

"And Rob isn't mentioned in any of these articles, along with his friend Murdo?"

"No, he isn't. I've checked very thoroughly."

"Then maybe this is a red-herring. Perhaps Rob wasn't involved at all, otherwise the details would have come out after the secret records had been declassified, wouldn't they? We'd know about it by now."

Bill shrugged. "Possibly, but it is odd we can't find any record of what your uncle *did* get up to." He sighed. "Of course, not all of the records were declassified."

"What do you mean?"

"I've read about it. There are still plenty of UK and US operations and activities from the Second World War which remain protected under the Official Secrets Act."

"Why on earth have these documents not yet been released? Its over seventy years since the war."

Bill leant forward. "Because they relate to activities that consecutive governments have felt are too sensitive to become common knowledge. They will involve the murkiest and least ethical elements of warfare."

"Good Lord," Joy put a hand to her neck. "I think you'd better order us both a large brandy, darling."

Chapter 34

Phil Boag opened his front door, adopting an expression of mock surprise. "I'm starting to think you can't stay away from me right now."

Dani grinned. "Thanks for agreeing to meet. I know you're busy."

"That's the thing with working from home," Phil called over his shoulder as he led her through to the kitchen, "everyone thinks they can drop by whenever they like."

Dani's expression became more serious. She shrugged out of her jacket and perched on a stool. "We've identified the second body we found on Ghiant."

"Oh, aye?" Phil brought over a pot of coffee and two mugs.

"He was a student who went missing from GCU back in March 2008."

Phil frowned, a flash of recognition crossed his face. "An Asian lad?"

"That's right. Adnan Mahtam. You and Matt Currie handled the report of his disappearance."

"Shit. I'm sorry he wound up dead."

"Alice has read the reports, but I want to hear about the case from you."

"The parents came in to report their son missing. He was supposed to be staying with fellow students on campus but hadn't turned up. To be honest, we didn't take it too seriously to begin with. He'd only been gone a night. He was twenty years old and living the student lifestyle. We told his folks to wait for another few hours."

"Then Mr and Mrs Mahtam came back."

Phil looked sheepish. "Yeah, it was over twenty-four hours by then since he'd been meant to touch base at the friend's place. I went to the uni and interviewed his tutors. We found out he was last seen at a lecture a couple of days before. I interviewed the family at their house in Sighthill. That's when the sister mentioned that Adnan attended the Baird Street Mosque."

"And this set the alarm bells ringing."

"It was all we'd been living and breathing the previous few months. When I got back to the station, I passed on the information to Juliet."

"What did she say?"

"Juliet instructed us to assume it could be connected to our anti-terrorism investigation. She suggested it was most likely Adnan was in training somewhere and hadn't informed his parents. It happened quite often. We were on high alert for another attack."

"Did you follow the usual procedure in a missing persons investigation?"

Phil crossed his arms protectively. "Yes, we did. Matt looked at the CCTV tapes from the campus. The boy wasn't in any of them. I interviewed his friends and family, put a trace on his phone. His debit cards were never used. Every avenue drew a blank. But the idea he'd taken off to Pakistan never sat right with me. They usually left a note in those situations, some kind of justification for their actions."

"Did you view the CCTV tapes yourself?"

Phil crinkled his face. "No, Matt did it. I wasn't going to do the job twice."

"You took his word for it?"

"Yes. Hang on, Dani, what's going on here? Are

the parents of this boy lodging a complaint?"

Dani shook her head sadly. "They should have done so many years back, but no, they aren't. This is more serious than that. What about Kerr Travis? Did he intervene in the investigation in any way?"

Phil considered this carefully. "I don't recall him getting involved at all." He put down his cup with a clatter as a recollection returned. "In fact, Kerr wasn't in the department that week the report came in. He was on some kind of terrorism awareness course. It was all about how terrorist groups were using social media to radicalise new recruits. That was a new thing back then."

Dani felt her blood run cold, a tingle crept along her arms to her fingertips. "How long did you keep looking for the boy?"

"I was checking in with the family for a few weeks. The bank kept me informed if there was any movement in his account. There never was. I passed his information to all the misper agencies in Glasgow. Listen, Dani, I carried on with the investigation for longer than I was meant to. Juliet insisted Adnan would have been smuggled over to Pakistan. She even had his details placed on a UN watchlist in Afghanistan."

"But he wasn't there. The boy never left Scotland. Someone must have bundled him into a vehicle and transported him to a remote island, where he was beaten to death and buried in the mud. This happened in *Scotland*, Phil. Not some oppressive, war-torn state."

Phil stood up. "It's awful, I know. But I did everything I could at the time. I followed all the procedures."

Dani reached up and took his arm. "I know you did. I'm sorry. I just wonder if the others were as thorough. DC Currie was always a lazy sod. I expect if Juliet told him he didn't need to view all those hours of CCTV tape, that she'd take care of it, he'd not have argued too much."

"But why the hell would Juliet do that? It was a low-level missing persons case. They surely had more important things to worry about?"

"I don't know yet precisely why she did it. But the possible reasons are almost too horrific to comprehend."

Chapter 35

There'd been no movement at the property for a couple of hours. Dani had reclined the seat in her car and was listening to a local radio station, the windows securely shut against the chill.

If Lorraine Travis was at home, she'd have surely clocked Dani's presence outside by now. The estate was so quiet, any unusual vehicle on the road was bound to be noticed.

It didn't seem worth interviewing Kerr's wife again. Dani didn't think she knew anything about her husband's activities, either now or a decade ago. She'd seen no sign of their grown-up children either.

Dani closed her eyes for a moment. She was running through the information Phil had given her. After visiting his house, she'd gone straight to Pitt Street and looked up all the professional courses that ran in the March of 2008. She identified the one Kerr could have been attending. It took place in a hotel in Lanark from the 10th to the 14th. There were several seminars listed in the itinerary, spread across the four days.

A heavy weight slammed against the car and made Dani open her eyes with a jerk. A face was pressed against the passenger window, enclosed in a dark hoodie. She sat up and release the locks. The man wrenched open the door and dropped into the seat beside her.

"What the hell are you doing here?" He growled, pulling the hood back from his thick, dark hair.

"I could ask you the same thing, Kerr."

"This is my house. I keep an eye on it from time to time." Kerr's face was little changed. He was still handsome, but the years had etched deeper lines around his eyes and mouth. "You being here could put my family in danger."

Dani shifted round. "That's bullshit. Your family are perfectly safe for as long as your cover isn't blown. I don't even know what your assignment is."

Kerr stared out of the front windscreen. "It's a long way from here."

"Then what are you really doing back in Paisley? Worried I'm about to find out something about you that might end your career? Put you in prison, maybe?"

Kerr twisted in the seat, his expression a snarl. "You're supposed to be finding the bastard that butchered Juliet, not digging around into our professional conduct. Whose side are you on?"

Dani could feel her anger bubbling up. "What happened to the boy who was buried on Ghiant? You were out of Glasgow when he went missing. Juliet tried to stall the investigation into his disappearance. Did you really attend that conference in Lanark? It will be easy enough for me to check with the hotel, contact witnesses who took the course from other divisions."

Without warning, Kerr reached across her and pulled her close to his face. With his free hand, he jabbed a hard metal object into her side. Dani felt her stomach churn.

"I strongly suggest you don't," He rasped into her ear. "Juliet was one of us. You need to find who killed her. That should be your priority. If you start investigating me, I'll be taken off the undercover work and be as exposed as she was."

Dani breathed deeply, trying to calm herself down. "Put away the gun, Kerr. We're sitting outside your house. Don't do anything stupid."

The man yanked the gun away, stuffing it into the waistband of his trousers. He lessened his grip on her. "You're right. It's just that this is such a mess, Dani. Since you told me Juliet was murdered, I haven't slept."

"Did Juliet contact you before she was killed? Did you know you were in danger?" Dani shuffled higher up in the seat. "Is that why you signed up for the undercover operations? To keep yourself safe?"

Kerr's mouth was set in a grim line. "I haven't felt safe since that bomb exploded in Roydon Road. My whole life tilted on its axis that day. The things I saw, Dani. I could never have burdened you with them."

She leant in closer. "I thought I knew everything about you, Kerr. But to kidnap a young man, tie him up and then what? Beat him until he told you where his friends were making their bombs? But what if he didn't have a clue? Was just an innocent young lad who worshipped his religion in the wrong place at the wrong time." She examined his face closely. "He couldn't tell you anything, could he? So, you beat him in the stomach and chest until the lifeblood had seeped from his young body, and he couldn't identify you to anyone else. Was that it?"

Kerr brought his hands up to his face. "It wasn't like that. The whole thing was a cock-up. The boys tried to escape. Two of them took the boat. We needed to get Adnan to tell us where they were planning to go."

Dani shook her head in disbelief. "You mean there were more of them? It wasn't just Adnan Mahtam you took to the island?"

"*Of course* there were others. Why do you think I'm running so scared? Why do you think Juliet is dead? We contacted one another every few months after she retired. She used to drive to meet me somewhere, depending on where my undercover work took me. The rest of the time we wrote, sending messages to a post office box in Central Station. In the final note I received, she said she was being watched. Her words sounded panicky. We knew they'd find us eventually, but we still weren't prepared."

"What about Sean Ballater? What role did he play in all this? Because he's dead too."

Kerr let his head loll forward. "Sean and Juliet were lovers, but their relationship was more about making someone pay for what we'd witnessed together. Sean married his mousy girlfriend and bought the farm up on Nabb. The fishing was a great cover. But he was really there to give us access to the island. Sean was the ferryman."

Dani felt the sadness wash over her. "You have to come in to Pitt Street with me and tell Chief Superintendent McNair all this. It's the only way we can protect you."

He grunted. "I'll go away for murder, Dani."

"Adnan's parents deserve to know what happened to their son."

Kerr lifted his head. "That boy may have been ignorant of what those people were up to, but the others certainly weren't. Adnan Mahtam associated with people who were happy to commit mass murder – to target *children*, for Christ's sake."

"Since when does that carry a death sentence? Since when do we interview suspects using intimidation and violence? It makes the situation worse, Kerr. I can't believe you don't see that."

"It's a war, Dani. The realities don't fit with your neat rules and regulations. If we don't get tough, they will win."

"If we interrogate innocent young boys, beat them

to death and try to hide our crimes, then they've won already, Kerr. We've lost our values."

"I won't go to prison. I'd rather take my chances out there."

Dani reached across to grab his jacket, but Kerr already had the door open. He jumped out of the car and disappeared down a side street, before she had the chance to get her key into the ignition.

Chapter 36

Andy was the first to share his information with the team. "Gail Ballater claims she's never heard of Adnan Mahtam, or Kerr Travis for that matter. I was inclined to believe her."

Dani nodded. "Travis suggested that his marriage to Gail was simply a cover, to allow him to live here without drawing suspicion."

"But he remained on Nabb for all these years," Alice added. "There must have been more to it."

"Perhaps there was," DI Peyton added. "They bought the cottage and the land. Ballater's father had been a fisherman. He chose a life he didn't mind living."

"Ballater supplemented that living by taking payments for ferrying folk to the smaller islands at any time of the day or night and for any purpose." Andy felt his cheeks redden. "I expect he got that idea from the job he did for Lowther and Travis." He thought back to the night they sailed out to Ghiant with the Hutchisons. Ballater had gone to have a smoke in the ruins of the post office whilst they got on with their business. He wondered how often the man had done that exact same thing in the past.

"There is an alert out for DS Travis," Dani explained. "Because of his undercover work, the search for him is strictly low-key. There will be no coverage in the press. If his real identity gets splashed across the nationals, there are other officers currently undercover whose lives will be at risk."

"Won't that make it harder to trace him?" DI Peyton looked annoyed.

Dani sighed. "Yes, it will. It seems that Travis has been very canny at saving his own arse."

Alice stepped forward. "Juliet Lowther left herself far more exposed. Ballater and Travis had disappeared into the woodwork, but her whereabouts were easy for anyone to trace."

"Retiring from the force and moving to Fort William did make her less conspicuous. I believe she ditched her plans to move her mother in with her because she feared retribution for what they did to the boys on that island. Her mother was safer in the rest home. Recently, she had herself confirmed into the church. I think she was ready for what was to come. Perhaps she was ready to make peace with her sins." Dani tried to feel sympathy for her old friend, but the emotion didn't come.

Peyton looked thoughtful. "Juliet told Kerr she was being watched. She kept her car in a secret location, presumably so she could move about unobserved. But someone found her in the end, following her to that carpark in Mallaig. Or enticing her there."

"You told us Travis admitted there were more young men on the island when Adnan was killed. Do we know how many? At least one of them managed to escape, so they must have washed up somewhere along the west coast." Andy addressed the DCI.

"Travis didn't give me any more details."

Alice got to her feet. "But it means the ones who escaped had a boat, the one they stole from Ballater and Kerr. Is it possible they still have that boat now?"

Dani nodded. "It's entirely possible." She rubbed her temples. "I don't think Travis is going to talk, even if Glasgow Division manage to track him down.

We need to check all records of missing persons from the Glasgow area reported in the Spring of 2008. Our young men must be among them."

"There could be dozens of reports," Andy lamented.

"Then we'd better get started," Dani added, with determination in her tone.

Chapter 37

It was nearly dark by the time Dani emerged from the Nabb town hall. She was fighting to keep her eyelids open, she could feel the grit forming painful deposits under their soft skin.

The evening was mild, the wind just a gentle breeze. As Dani approached the entrance of the Gordon Hotel, she felt an arm suddenly grip her coat sleeve. She spun around, ready to floor whoever was trying to intercept her path.

"Bill! For heaven's sake! You can't grab me like that. I could have knocked you to the ground."

The man looked put-out. "Well, that wouldn't have been very friendly, DCI Bevan. It's just you've been away for so long and I've got something very important to talk to you about."

Dani wondered if it was as important as a multiple murder inquiry. She glanced at her watch. "We could share a nightcap in the bar."

His face lit up. "Oh, marvellous. I could really do with a brandy. I've been waiting out here for you for hours."

Dani said nothing, simply allowing him to lead the way inside.

Bill returned from the bar with a brandy and a whisky and soda.

"Joy and I have been doing some research into the island. We thought it might help."

"Okay." Dani sipped her drink, the warmth of the whisky was welcome.

"Well, it was more into Joy's uncle and aunt."

Dani could sense Bill's steady voice lulling her into a peaceful state. She relaxed into the high-backed leather armchair and listened, as he recounted the information they'd gleaned about Robert Rushbrooke, who's war record wasn't as straightforward as they'd first believed. The story was a distant and mildly intriguing one until Bill said something that made her sit bolt upright.

"Rob's service record is still classified?" Dani repeated.

"I don't actually know that, but I'm assuming it must be the case, as he clearly worked with SOE, yet his whereabouts during the war aren't recorded in any of the online archives."

"Then it probably won't be possible for you and Joy to find out any more. I don't know much about the SOE, but I'm aware the operatives often worked abroad."

"That tended to be the foreign nationals whom the allies had recruited. There were many overseas agents operating in eastern Europe and in France, most notably." Bill finished his brandy. "No, I have been considering this carefully since we found out about Rob's links to the secret services." He leant forward conspiratorially. "I think Rob's posting was a little closer to home."

Dani narrowed her eyes, she wasn't in the mood for guessing games.

"I believe Rob was based on Ghiant itself during the war."

Dani put down her glass. "I thought Rob met Joy's aunt at an army base somewhere and they returned to Ghiant *after* the war was over."

Bill waved his hand dismissively. "That was the story, yes. But we found out that Ghiant was used by the army as a lookout station during the war."

"That doesn't sound very top secret."

"No, that's my point exactly. What Rob was up to had to be so sensitive that the details still cannot be released into the public domain. There are only a few things that can mean. I don't believe they were detonating nuclear devices on Ghiant, so it only leaves a handful of other possibilities."

Dani's mind was ticking over.

"Ghiant is a very remote island with few inhabitants. Rob knew the place like the back of his hand. His family's farm was on the island, giving access to numerous outhouses."

Dani was thinking about her current case. Lowther and Travis had chosen Ghiant as a place to take their terrorist suspects because it was in the middle of nowhere and nobody lived on it. Yet Ballater could get them to the island with relative ease by boat.

"You think they were interrogating people on Ghiant during the war?"

Bill nodded. "I suspect so. It would have gone against the Geneva Convention, which all countries had to follow in the war years. But we know the Germans did it, and the Japanese, of course."

"Who would the British army have wanted to interrogate?"

Bill shrugged his shoulders. "Top ranking prisoners of war, defectors from the axis countries, people found spying for the enemy. There are many possibilities in wartime."

"I thought the Brits treated their POWs very well. That's what my dad always told me."

"Yes, we did. But there were still internment camps across the country for foreign nationals. And there was a war on, Danielle. There may have been times when more drastic action was necessary. There were moments when defeat to Germany seemed like a very real danger. This is when Rob's role would have been at its most crucial."

"Do you really think the Isle of Ghiant was used as a secret location to interrogate the enemy during World War Two? It seems like it would be impossible to keep that a secret for all these years?"

"If the people involved took that secret to the grave, and the documents relating to its use have remained classified, I think it's entirely plausible. There will be people who know, of course. There always are. But they will be in important positions of power and will not want the country to be embarrassed by the release of the truth now."

Dani sat in silence. She tried to make out the shape of the island through the window of the lounge bar, but it was too dark outside and the lights of the hotel were too brightly reflected in the glass. Had Juliet known the secret history of Ghiant? Was it something she discovered when she had security clearance to investigate counter-terrorism?

Did this knowledge give her the idea of taking their own recalcitrant suspects to Ghiant, a place remote and isolated, where in wartime, interrogation had been given some kind of legitimacy? Hadn't Kerr described the situation following the bus bombing as a 'war'. Perhaps Juliet saw herself as an heir to the agents who operated on Ghiant in the 1940s. This could well have been her justification.

She suddenly realised Bill was still talking.

"This wasn't the information Joy wanted to hear. Her memories of the summer she spent on the island in the 1950s were of an idyllic existence. Now we suspect the government wanted Rob there, as a caretaker for the place, to guard any evidence that might have remained of their activities. It's why they received compensation in the end." Bill sighed. "But Joy's not taken it as badly as I thought. She wants to return home to Louise and the boys. In fact, she's keen to find out more about her own father's role in the war. I think she believes she was perhaps too judgmental of him as a young girl. Kenneth wasn't exciting, you see. He was a rather dour man, as I recall. But I believe Joy feels she should give his memory a little more attention."

"I'm glad," Dani stated flatly. "I'd like to think some glimmer of good has come out of all this."

Chapter 38

Matt Currie had left the police force a couple of years previously. The growing emphasis on paperwork didn't suit him. Since then, he'd taken a series of jobs in security. Currently, he was a night security guard at one of the major hotels in the city.

Phil Boag hadn't really kept in touch with Matt, only by way of the annual Christmas card. But he found the man still living at the address where he'd been when they worked together. Matt's wife filled him in on the rest.

The lobby of the Cadogan Hotel was brightly lit by the staggering number of chandeliers suspended from the ceiling. Matt wasn't difficult to spot. His bulky form was squeezed into a smart black suit. An earpiece protruded conspicuously from the side of his closely shaved head.

Phil approached him without preamble. "Matt. long time no see."

The man looked Phil up and down. It seemed to take him a while to process the information his eyes were giving him. "*Phil Boag*? Christ, it's been years."

Phil met the man's gaze and fixed him with a stare. "We need to talk."

"I'm at work, pal." Matt glanced nervously around at the staff on the reception desk.

"Then take a break."

He examined his watch, as if he'd only just learnt how to interpret the position of its dials. "Okay, I could take my break in five."

"I'll meet you at the café across the street. Don't

keep me waiting."

When Matt pushed through the door of the greasy spoon, he had a padded jacket pulled on over his swanky suit. Phil had ordered them both a mahogany brown mug of tea.

Matt shovelled sugar into his. "What do you want to talk about?" He kept his gaze fixed on the chipped Formica.

Phil leant forward. "Adnan Mahtam."

"Who?"

Phil nearly laughed. "He was a twenty year old student who went missing from GCU in March 2008. We handled the case, remember?"

"Oh, him."

"Yes, *him*. Only his body was found last week. He'd been beaten to death, within days of him going missing. His body was buried on an island off Skye."

Matt finally looked up. "What the hell? We thought he'd gone off to join the Taliban."

Phil shook his head slowly. "You and Juliet thought that. I never did."

"We conducted a thorough investigation, Phil. The file will show that."

"I'm not here to make sure we've both covered our arses." Phil's expression was one of disgust. "I want to know why you lied to me."

"About what?"

Phil wasn't a man to lose his temper easily, but he could feel the anger brewing. "I asked you to examine the CCTV footage from around the campus and surrounding streets on the afternoon Adnan went missing. You told me he wasn't on any of the footage. Was that true?"

Matt seemed suddenly engrossed in the actions of the waitress behind the counter who was noisily frying eggs.

Phil brought his fist down on the table. Tea slopped over the lips of their cups and pooled around the bases. "Tell me the truth!"

A few fellow customers glanced briefly in their direction, quickly returning to their meals. It was late, and Phil imagined this establishment probably experienced its fair share of nutters.

"I started to. Then I passed the footage on to Juliet." Matt's voice sounded weak.

"Why did you do that?"

"Because I saw something on one of the tapes that I wanted to clarify with her."

"Okay, I'm listening."

"She told me that what I'd seen was part of a classified counter-terrorism investigation. The DI claimed you'd not got clearance to view the material."

"And you didn't smell bullshit?"

"Lowther was the boss. What else could I do?"

Phil tried to recall the intensity of the atmosphere in the department back then. Everyone was watching their backs. But he still lacked sympathy. "What did you see, Matt? Lowther is dead now and Kerr Travis is on the run. You're under no obligation to keep their dirty secrets."

Matt made eye contact. "I'd watched a few hours of tape. Then I finally spotted the lad. He was wearing that blue sports jacket his parents told us about. Adnan was heading along Kennedy Street, towards the newsagents. Then, two figures stepped out from a side street and talked to him. One of them was kinda gripping his arm. They turned as they led him out of sight of the camera. I caught a look at both their faces at that point." He cleared his throat. "It was DI Lowther and DS Travis."

"Bloody hell."

"I didn't know what to do," his voice had become

shrill. "I showed it to Lowther. She said the boy was known to them, he had associations with the Roydon Road bombers. They'd spoken to him that afternoon. But when she and Travis left the lad, he was alive and well. Lowther reckoned they'd shaken him up with their questions and that's why he'd taken off that day to a training camp somewhere. For safety, she said."

"Why didn't you tell me this at the time?"

"Lowther said it was confidential. She said the Mahtam's missing persons' report would complicate their counter-terrorism investigation. If that tape fell into the wrong hands, their operation would all have been for nothing."

Phil shook his head. "Those bastards. Who the hell did they think they were?"

Matt's face had gone pale. "They weren't the ones who killed the lad, were they?"

Phil sighed. "You were a detective for over a decade, Matt. I'll leave you to work that one out."

"Holy shit."

Phil got to his feet. "I need you to walk into Pitt Street station first thing tomorrow morning and make an official statement to a DC called Dan Clifton. He'll be expecting you. And don't worry, Matt. I don't think you'll get into any trouble."

"It's okay, I want to do it. Set the record straight."

Phil sprinkled coins on the table and headed for the door, hoping he'd never have to set eyes on the man again.

Chapter 39

As they approached the block of flats, Dani sensed something different about the place. She couldn't put her finger on exactly what it was.

DS Forrest punched in the code on the exterior door and led Dani and Andy up the stairs to Juliet Lowther's flat. The landing was as silent as it had been when Dani was first there.

On this second visit, Dani understood more about the woman who had lived out her last few years in the apartment. Juliet was a woman who knew her card was marked. She had kept her life simple, always looking over her shoulder.

Andy walked in and out of the compact rooms. "Is there somewhere else Lowther might have kept the rest of her stuff – there must be trinkets from her late mother, that kind of thing. This place is clean as a whistle."

DS Forrest shook his head. "Apart from the car, there was no evidence she kept anything away from this place. One of my team checked all the local storage companies and even those down in Glasgow."

"Her brother told me that most of their mother's furniture was sold when she went into residential care," Dani explained. "Juliet insisted Charles should take any jewellery for his daughters. There wasn't much left after that."

"Sounds like Juliet was clearing the decks." Andy glanced about him at the stark surroundings.

Dani went to the sink and looked out of the window, down onto the street. The view was obscured by an old-fashioned net curtain. She pulled it aside. A realisation abruptly dawned.

Dani spun round and addressed DS Forrest. "When we arrived just now. There weren't any nets up at the windows of the flat downstairs. I'm sure there were when I was last here."

Forrest rubbed his forehead. "That's right. The old dear downstairs has moved out. I think her family have put her in a home. The landlord's cleared the whole flat out and is repainting. I spoke to him the other day. He's hoping to attract a younger couple to move in there. Especially with the status of this place in limbo. He could do with charging a higher rent. Young folk don't like nets."

Dani blinked rapidly. "Juliet wrote to Kerr Travis to tell him she thought she was being watched. The lady downstairs, she watched Juliet's movements, didn't she?"

Forrest grimaced. "Yes, she did. But only in a nosy old biddy type of way."

"Watching someone is watching someone," Andy added dryly.

"Can you talk to the landlord again?" Dani asked briskly. "I want every detail he can give you about the *old dear* who lived downstairs from Juliet Lowther."

*

They parked the car on the private strip of land on the outskirts of Mallaig where Lowther's abandoned green Ford Focus had been found. The place was overlooked by an imposing line of tall pine trees, making it a lonely spot that must have been dark by mid-afternoon.

Dani and Andy walked towards the port. The wind was whipping into shore, driving cold rain into their faces. The residential home they were heading for was next to the leisure centre, its sea view obscured by an ugly tall fence surrounding a marina.

The manager of the home took a perfunctory look at their ID cards before leading them to one of the rooms along a dingy ground floor corridor. He knocked loudly before leaving them to it.

Dani pushed open the door. A woman with wispy white hair was seated by the tiny window. A row of potted plants had been crammed onto the narrow sill, threatening to topple at any moment onto her head.

"Mrs Lykova. We are officers from the Glasgow police. We need to ask you some questions."

Her expression was confused. "What has happened? Is Anna okay?"

"Nothing has happened. May we take a seat?"

The lady nodded.

"We are investigating the death of Juliet Lowther. One of our officers has already spoken to you."

"Oh yes," she replied. "He came to my flat." Her face fell and a mist blurred her bright blue eyes. "I had to leave it. Anna said we could no longer afford the rent. I miss my garden."

"I'm sure you do." Andy looked disapprovingly around the small, dark room.

"You told DS Forrest that you watched Juliet from out of your front window, is that right?" Dani continued.

"That's right. I liked to take an interest in my neighbours. Juliet was on her own so it was my duty to check on her."

"Did you ever tell anyone about Juliet's movements, other than DS Forrest?"

Mrs Lykova shuffled uncomfortably in her chair. "I'm not supposed to say anything. I had a nice place to live and it was only a small thing to do in return."

Andy leant forward. "Well, you aren't living in that nice flat now, are you. They've moved you here, with no garden. I don't see why you can't tell us about it."

She let her eyes scan her miserable surroundings. "I didn't know that I wouldn't be able to stay there. I thought I'd done everything I was told."

"You *did* do everything you were told, I'm sure," Dani continued. "But this is a fine way to repay you."

She nodded. "Yes, I was very upset with Anna when she told me."

"Who is Anna?"

"My daughter, of course. Anna Aliyev. She lives with her husband in Fort William, not far from where I was." Her eyes misted again.

"Was it your daughter who wanted to know Juliet's movements. Was it her who you told?"

The lady paused for a moment and then replied. "Sometimes, yes. But most of the time I told Eric, my grandson. He was the one who came to visit most often. He helped me tend the garden. He had a key to the back door."

"Is that Eric Aliyev?" Andy clarified, making a note.

"Yes, he's been such a help to me since he returned."

"Where had he been?"

Mrs Lykova looked confused again. "He was fighting in an important war. For the honour of Kazakhstan, which is my homeland."

"Okay, how long was he away for?"

"A long time, many years. He was just a young man when he left. A good, meek boy, a religious boy. Eric came back a soldier. His cousin wasn't so lucky."

"What happened to him?"

"Marat was killed in the war. His mother was devastated. She never got over it."

"What does Eric do now he's back in Scotland?" Dani kept her tone gentle, cajoling.

"It hasn't been easy for him. Eric has been working on the ferry boats and driving taxi cabs, whatever work he could get."

"Where does he live?" Andy couldn't refrain from asking.

Mrs Lykova gestured towards the small window. "Eric is here in Mallaig. They said by moving I would be closer to him. But he hasn't visited once yet."

Chapter 40

The house was a seventies semi-detached with a garage to the side. Alice had placed a priority on the warrant to search the premises, but the document had still taken until the following morning to arrive. Dani just hoped that Mrs Lykova hadn't tipped her grandson off that they were looking for him.

It didn't seem as if she had. Dani saw a flicker of movement behind one of the bedroom windows as they stood outside. She gestured to a couple of DCs from Highlands and Islands that they should go around the back.

Andy stepped up to the door and leant on the bell. Perhaps Eric Aliyev had seen the officers entering his garden because he opened up, showing no indication he was about to do a bunk.

The man was tall and broad, with a head of curly dark hair which he wore to shoulder-length. "Come inside," he said courteously, with a soft Glaswegian burr to his accent.

The house was clean but sparsely furnished. Alice had already ascertained the property was rented by Aliyev from a local landlord with several other houses in the area.

They reached the living room and sat down. Eric dipped his head towards the two burly men standing guard on his patio. "Was that really necessary?"

"You are a suspect in a murder investigation, Mr Aliyev. I think it's entirely justified." Dani eyed him carefully. He was neatly dressed, in chinos and a roll-neck sweater. She already knew he was 31 years old and had spent the first 22 years of his life living in Glasgow.

"We spoke to your grandmother," Dani explained. "She told us where to find you. But I wouldn't be too hard on her, I don't believe she understood what she was doing."

"No, she wouldn't. My grandmother had no part in this, or any other member of my family. I acted entirely alone." He expression was resolute.

"What about your mother? Weren't you using Anna to collect information for you about Juliet Lowther?"

He shook his head vehemently. "My mother knew nothing either. Grandmother told her about Juliet, but it was me who wanted the information. To Anna, it was simply evidence of the nosiness of an inquisitive old lady."

Andy shifted his weight forward. "But your old Granny could be charged with accessory to murder. You did use the information Mrs Lykova gave you to murder Juliet Lowther, didn't you?"

"Leave her out of this. She's just a confused old woman!"

"*You* brought her into it, Eric. Can't you see that?"

Dani glanced around her. "We've got a warrant to search these premises. I'm particularly interested to see what's in your garage. Do you own a car?"

"No. I drive mini cabs sometimes for a friend. I use that if I need to get about."

"Then what's kept in the garage?"

Eric leant his tall, lean body against the frame of the patio door. "My boat."

Dani nodded to Andy, who stood and left the room. "My colleague will be calling in a forensic team to examine that boat. Even if it's been scrubbed clean, we'll still find evidence. Juliet must have bled an awful lot after you stabbed her. The blood would have gone everywhere."

Eric gazed out into the garden, where the two officers were seated on plastic garden chairs, sharing a cigarette. "I could have fled again, like I did back in 2008. But it didn't feel like the right thing to do this time. Anyway, there was nowhere to go. For me, the war is over."

"Tell me what happened."

"We were young students. Adnan studied at GCU and Marat and I had graduated from the technical college in Maryhill. We met Adnan at the mosque."

"On Baird Street?"

He nodded. "We became friends. Adnan was a quiet boy, like my cousin and I. We shared similar backgrounds. Our families were devout Muslims but we had been born in Scotland. All we wanted was the chance to get a good education and practice our religion in peace. We knew there were groups operating in our community who felt resentment towards the west. They were angry about the invasion of Afghanistan and Blair's illegal war in Iraq. We understood their grievances but never subscribed to the violence of their ideas. Not then, anyway."

Dani said nothing, allowing him to continue.

"When we were worshipping at the mosque one evening, DI Lowther and her henchman turned up."

"DS Travis."

"They marched us into a room and questioned us about the bombing, about what we knew of the boys who took the bombs to the bus station. Of course, we knew nothing about it. Adnan's father was a lecturer in law, so he understood something of our rights. He told us to say nothing, even to the simplest of questions. This seemed to infuriate them."

"They should never have questioned you outside a police station. You should have had lawyers present."

Eric laughed. "They did far worse. Our friends' houses were ransacked in the middle of the night. Children terrified out of their wits. I suppose we thought we could outsmart the police officers. We refused to open our mouths in their presence, we wouldn't even look at them, but kept our heads facing the floor. I could tell it made the male officer want to lash out at us."

"It probably encouraged them both to think you were hiding something."

"I realise that now. But back then we were young and cocky. We underestimated them."

"Adnan went missing on the 12th March. Did they take you and Marat on the same day?"

"Yes. They intercepted us as we walked home from prayers. A bag was put over our heads and we were bundled into the back of a van. The journey was long, several hours at least. We were alone in the back, so we could whisper to one another. That's how we knew Adnan was there too." He moved across the room and sat opposite Dani. "We finally stopped moving. The man, Travis, led us out of the van and into a boat. I could feel the motion as we climbed on board. Our hands were bound behind our backs and I could feel the metal barrel of his gun intermittently pressed into my flesh."

Dani recognised the feeling.

"It was once we were off the boat that the torture started. They waited until we were bound and gagged in a chair before the hoods were removed. I saw Travis then and another man."

"Sean Ballater."

"Yes, I found that out later. We were in a large barn. They interrogated us for several hours. Mostly it was beatings, but when they got really frustrated with us, Ballater brought in a pig's trough full of stagnant water. Travis tipped up our chairs so that our faces were submerged. He didn't lift us out until we were about to asphyxiate. The other man just stood and watched. I'll never forget it."

"Good God." Dani felt sick.

"There was no God present in that place. We were in hell for those few days."

"Are you okay to continue?"

Eric wiped away the beads of sweat that had broken out across his brow. "Those first few hours were the worst. When our captors were united. But as time went on, it became clear we didn't know anything. That's when Ballater started to panic. He was arguing with Travis, saying it was all a mistake, they weren't going to get any leads from us. Marat recognised their loss of resolve. He asked to go to the toilet. He said he was in pain. He worked on Ballater whenever he was watching us alone. Eventually, the man came across and untied him."

Dani imagined Ballater as the weak link, the one who was slowly coming to realise they'd kidnapped a group of innocent men.

"When they were out of the room, Marat turned on Ballater, he shoved him to the ground and kicked him in the head. The man was dazed or unconscious. It gave Marat enough time to come back into the barn and cut me loose. But within minutes we heard Travis return. He'd found Ballater on the ground." Eric's voice became distant. "We didn't have time to free Adnan. The decision to go has haunted me ever since. I know we left him to his death. He never returned to his parents. Our associates at the mosque could not trace him."

Dani needed to snap the man out of his guilt-ridden malaise. "How did you and Marat get off the island?"

"The sun was high in the sky. We'd totally lost track of time and it was lucky it wasn't dark. The island was small and we found the boat easily. I untied the ropes and pushed off, Marat dragged me aboard and we started the motor. I was convinced we would be wanted men. The whole of the Scottish police force would be out looking for us. So, we sailed for as long as there was daylight to guide us. We came ashore not far up the coast from here. We hid the boat amongst the foliage by the shore. My grandmother lived in Fort William then, so we hitch-hiked to her house."

"You never raised the alarm about Adnan?"

Eric lifted his arms in exasperation. "How could we? Adnan was being held by the British police. Who could we call upon to help him?"

Dani shook her head in sorrow at the evil committed by her one-time colleagues. They'd made a mockery of everything the police service stood for. "They beat him to death, trying to find out where the two of you were heading. His body was found in a shallow grave, just metres from the barn where you were kept."

Eric doubled over and sobbed. "Bastards! Why couldn't they have left him alone! He was just an innocent boy!"

"You should have reported it, Eric. When you returned to the UK. We could have punished the three of them properly, in a court of law."

Eric raised his gaze to meet hers. "I'm not the law-abiding, foolish boy I once was. Marat and I couldn't stay in Scotland, we feared the police were after us. We had no choice but to contact those very groups whose extremist views we had abhorred. These men got us passage to Pakistan, where there were camps on the border with Afghanistan where we could train to be soldiers. We fought with our comrades for years. Marat was killed in a skirmish with UN forces five months ago. I knew it was time to return. The war in Afghanistan had never been my cause, nor Marat's either. My duty was to find those who had caused the death of Marat and Adnan and bring them to justice."

Andy stepped into the room. "We've got something, Ma'am."

Dani stood up. "Okay. Let's finish this at the police station."

Chapter 41

Fort William police station was in the centre of the town. Eric Aliyev was waiting in one of the cells on the ground floor. Dani wanted Alice and Grant Peyton to be able to join them for the interviews. They'd contributed so much to solving the case. A car had been sent to pick them up from their ferry.

Andy carried a couple of coffees into the corridor where Dani was seated. She accepted one of the cups gratefully.

"I've been on the phone to Gail Ballater. She confirmed that her husband had a boat stolen in the spring of 2008. She wanted to report it to the police, but Sean refused. He said it would just have been kids."

"Does the boat in Aliyev's garage match the one that went missing?"

"From Gail's description, I'd say so. But the forensic evidence will be the most compelling factor. When the techs shone their ultra-violet lights around that garage, the walls were dripping with blood stains."

Dani shuddered. "I don't think Eric is going to resist the charges. These murders were performed as a form of martyrdom."

"Will he receive any mitigation because of what those bastards did to him and the other boys?"

"I honestly don't know, Andy. This is outside my experience. We're in brand new territory."

Andy sat down, cradling the cardboard cup in his hands. "Bill and Joy are back home in Falkirk."

"Thank Christ for that," Dani muttered. "Let's hope they stay there, for a while, at least."

Andy laughed, nearly spilling the hot coffee in his lap.

A WPC put her head around the door. "DI Peyton and Mann have just arrived in reception, Ma'am."

Dani got up. "Thanks," she replied. "Let's get this interview started."

*

James had a bottle of wine gripped in his hand. Dani had a bunch of flowers. The bouquet was an elaborate arrangement, one she'd had individually prepared at a local florist. She wanted it to look as if they'd made a special effort.

Fiona answered the door. "Come inside, Phil's just taking the joint out of the oven."

As they were led along the hallway, Dani noticed that a teenage girl was spread out across one of the sofas, watching the large TV in the dark.

"Oh, Maisie's home for the weekend, I hope you don't mind."

"Of course we don't," Dani replied with feeling. In fact, the sight of Maisie filled her with a joy she wasn't expecting.

Phil beamed as they entered the room. The smell from the rack of lamb was sublime. "A conciliatory meal, to make up for my inadequacies in the Mahtam case."

Dani handed the flowers to Fiona and stepped forward to wrap her former colleague in an embrace. "You have nothing to be sorry for, Phil. Nobody could have predicted what Lowther and Travis were planning. You were one of the good guys back then and always will be."

"Steady on," James added with a wink. "Put down that man and help me pour the wine."

Dani waited until the meal was over and James had retreated with Fiona into the lounge, where he'd expressed a wish to examine a new piece of artwork she'd bought. The DCI could almost believe they were tactfully leaving her and Phil alone.

She turned to her host. "Travis has finally been found. His wife called the police when he turned up at the house."

"At least she didn't cover for him."

"The disciplinary board handling his case told Lorraine what he did to those boys. She wasn't impressed. Their son is that age now."

Phil sighed heavily. "I still can't believe it. We worked with Travis. We had no idea he was a monster."

Dani said nothing. She'd done more than worked with him, she'd shared his bed, imagined for a while she'd loved him.

"Have they set a trial date for Aliyev yet?"

"I think it will be delayed until after the investigation into Travis. The two cases are so closely related."

"Why did Eric target Juliet first and kill her so brutally? Surely Travis is the real villain in all this?"

"I'm not so sure. Juliet planned the whole thing. She was there in Glasgow when the boys were taken. Although it wasn't her who actually tortured them, it was Juliet who tidied up after it all went wrong. Travis is already trying to shift the blame onto her. Ballater called her after Marat and Eric stole the boat. Juliet had to come up and rescue them. She chartered a boat to get them off the island and helped them bury the body. She was as guilty as they were."

"Why did Juliet go and meet Eric Aliyev in Mallaig? She must have known it was dangerous for her to meet with any stranger, especially alone."

'Eric had been observing Juliet's comings and goings for several months. He moved his grandmother into the flat below Lowther's once he'd found out her address. He knew everything about her. The appointments with her clients and her newly found religion. She'd been visiting the priest every Sunday to prepare for Confirmation. According to Eric's testimony, this gave him an idea. He called Juliet and told her they needed to talk. Eric was open with her about who he was. He explained his religious faith meant he had to forgive her if she was truly sorry. She claimed she was and they agreed to meet."

"At the car-park in Mallaig?"

"Old habits didn't die so easily for Juliet. She chose a spot without CCTV cameras. I suppose so she could deny the meeting took place if she needed to. But it meant her car wasn't located for over a week. Eric spoke in an impassioned way to her when they met that afternoon. Told her that his forgiveness and her penitence would release them both. He took her to his house so they could talk further. Eric was a highly trained soldier. Once inside, he overpowered her and squeezed her neck until she was unconscious. He dragged her into the garage and stabbed her to death."

"Did he keep the body at his place?"

"Only for a day. Eric knew Juliet had no appointments with clients for the remainder of that week. He was aware of her routines. He disposed of her pay-as-you-go mobile, which she used only really to contact Travis. He wrapped the body in plastic sheets and waited until after dark to launch the boat. It was a voyage he was only too familiar with."

"Dumping her body on Ghiant, in the barn where they had been tortured must have been a sign. Because by leaving her identification on her, it meant he was more likely to be found." Phil stirred sugar into his coffee.

"Killing her was a tribute to Adnan and Marat. It wouldn't have made any sense if her body hadn't been left on the island where it all began."

"Ballater must have been easy to find. He had stayed so close to Ghiant."

"Yes, Eric already knew where Sean Ballater was. All he needed to do was ask a few questions around the harbour in Nabb. Eric could sail his boat into any of the small islets around that coast and ambush his target."

"I can't believe that Travis was left alone. He was the one most responsible for what happened to those poor boys."

"It shows what a clever bastard he was. By going deep undercover, Kerr Travis kept himself protected. Eric had no way of finding him. But he'll feel the full force of the law now."

Dani looked up to see Fiona and James, standing quite motionless in the doorway, listening. She straightened up guiltily. "I'm sorry, we shouldn't be talking about this stuff at a social occasion. It's unforgivable."

Fiona smiled. "Don't worry, Dani. Talk as much as you like. I haven't seen Phil look so energised by anything since you came back on the scene, asking for his help with this case."

James stalked across the room and took Dani's hand. "They're never happier than when they're on the job, these cops. It's really best for us to simply accept it Fiona."

"But Phil isn't a detective any longer," she commented wryly.

"Once a cop, always a cop, my dear." James took the edge off his words with a grin. "Now, shall I open another bottle?"

If you enjoyed this novel, please take a few moments to write a brief review. Reviews really help to introduce new readers to my books and this allows me to keep on writing.

Many thanks,

Katherine.

If you would like to find out more about my books and read my reviews and articles then please visit my blog, TheRetroReview at:

www.KatherinePathak.wordpress.com

To find out about new releases and special offers follow me on Twitter:

@KatherinePathak

Most of all, thanks for reading!

Made in the USA
San Bernardino, CA
15 December 2017